MURDERS IN SILK

by Asa Bordages
writing as Mike Teagle

Black Gat Books • Eureka California

MURDERS IN SILK

Published by Black Gat Books
A division of Stark House Press
1315 H Street
Eureka, CA 95501, USA
griffinskye3@sbcglobal.net
www.starkhousepress.com

MURDERS IN SILK
Published and copyright © 1938 by Hillman-Curl, Inc.,
New York, as by "Mike Teagle." Reprinted in paperback
by Lion Books, New York, 1951.

All rights reserved under International and
Pan-American Copyright Conventions.

ISBN: 979-8-88601-026-8

Cover design by Jeff Vorzimmer, ¡caliente!design, Austin, Texas
Text design by Mark Shepard, shepgraphics.com
Cover art by Ed Moritz

PUBLISHER'S NOTE:
This is a work of fiction. Names, characters, places and
incidents are either the products of the author's imagination or
used fictionally, and any resemblance to actual persons, living
or dead, events or locales, is entirely coincidental.
Without limiting the rights under copyright reserved above, no
part of this publication may be reproduced, stored, or
introduced into a retrieval system or transmitted in any form
or by any means (electronic, mechanical, photocopying,
recording or otherwise) without the prior written permission of
both the copyright owner and the above publisher of the book.

First Stark House Press/Black Gat Edition: April 2023

PART ONE
Which is related by Tiberius Bixby,
son of Zebediah Bixby

Chapter One

The first thing I noticed about the girl in the red calot was that she was an independent wench. She wore sheer black stockings and ignored the mirrors along the passageway to the Long Island Railroad level of the Pennsylvania Station. I noticed these circumstances with approval, especially the stockings.

I still didn't know why I was there, though, so I ambled over to the Information Desk. Maybe the Long Island Railroad could tell me.

"What day is it?" I said.

The young man behind the desk seemed to have sudden trouble with his adenoids. He deliberated the question at length before committing himself.

"Monday," he said.

"I mean, is it by any chance the thirteenth of June?"

"Yes, mister," he said. He seemed to be pained about something. He said confidentially, "It's 1948, too."

"Thanks, but I know what year it is."

He looked as though he doubted it, but I didn't make anything of it. A lot of people doubted us Bixbys knew what year it was. Pa says sometimes he does, too, and that's the only thing that ever gives him any hope for his children. He says he prays every night to be delivered from the kind of folks who always know the date. They're bound to be so insanely sane that they disapprove of the excessive use of Irish whiskey.

I felt a lot better when I learned it was June thirteenth. I'd been worried when my sister Messalina telephoned me that Pa wanted me to come home at once and then had hung up without explaining why. All the way from my apartment in Jane Street to the station, I felt that something must be wrong with the old man, for he always said that the longer I stayed away from Scraffton Station, the more sense I showed. It probably wasn't such a bad place when it was the Bixbys' cow pasture, but now it's a citadel of Long Island commuters and the Culbertson System. It's got a war memorial, a Chamber of Commerce and the proud record of having voted six to one for Landon. There are also other symptoms of intellectual arteriosclerosis. Pa couldn't stand the place any more than I could, but at sixty-five or so he said Messalina was the only person he'd ever found who ran a house the way he wanted it run, so he lived at home.

Pa didn't leave the rambling old house a dozen times a year, spending his days with a bottle and his books in the library on the second floor, still deluding himself with the idea that someday he would re-edit Gibbon's *Decline and Fall of the Roman Empire*. On the rare occasions when he did go out, he usually came to New York for a binge with me and a long lecture on how smart I was to stay away from home, even though I had to press agent a burlesque show to do it. So, naturally, when Messalina told me he wanted me to come home at once, I was plenty worried. I thought maybe he was dying. But learning the date explained everything. For June thirteenth is Pa's birthday, the only day in the year he allows himself to get sentimental about his children. He says that on his birthday he exercises every man's inalienable right to make a fool of himself.

MURDERS IN SILK

"The story is fast, slick, exciting and altogether an outstanding example of the tough trend; it also contains additional features in the way of character and real amusement. If you must have a ten-minute egg, read *Murders in Silk*."
—Will Cuppy, *Books*

"Good-natured cynicism, a clever plot well told, and a seventy-year-old chronic alcoholic make this book a feature of the mystery season. Three murders… and a wholly surprising denouement are some of the other factors that entitle this story to high praise." —*Boston Transcript*

"…well-drawn characters, good dialogue, an abundance (probably an overabundance) of violent action, and moves at a breakneck pace." —Bill Pronzini

Asa Bordages Bibliography
(1906-1986)

The Glass Lady (William Godwin, 1932;
  Lion Books, 1951)
There Shall Be Laughter (William Godwin, 1934)

As Mike Teagle

Death Over San Silvestro (Hillman-Curl, 1936)
Murders in Silk (Hillman-Curl, 1938;
  Lion Books, 1951)

After I learned the date, I went to a liquor store and bought a birthday present for Pa. I got him a couple of bottles of John Jameson's, that being his idea of the epitome of laudable demonstrations of filial affection. I hurried through the train gates with my package and headed for the smoker. That was when I saw the girl in the red calot again. She was standing on the platform talking to a scrawny little guy in a greenish suit. They seemed to be worried about something.

In case you don't know, a calot is a brimless little hat that looks like half of a round bombshell with the fuse sticking up on top. She was smart to wear that kind of a hat. She was dark and small, wearing a trim blue suit, and her black hair curled out from under the calot in Gypsy Rose Lee bangs. She didn't notice me as I went by, but the lug gave me a fishy stare. I couldn't help hearing what she was saying as I passed.

"Nothing can go wrong," she said. "He's got to bring it."

It was too early in the afternoon for the train to be crowded. I took the third seat from the back of the smoker and settled down behind my paper. The girl in the red calot came in and took a seat about midway up the car. Fish Eye trailed in after the girl, but he didn't sit with her. He took a seat across the aisle and lit a cigar. They were pretending they didn't know each other. There were a dozen or fifteen people in the car, and I wondered which of them was supposed to be taken in by the pretense and why. I even stood up to look over the bunch, but I couldn't get a hint. None of the others seemed to notice Fish Eye or the girl. Yet the act the lug and the dark girl were putting on must have been for somebody's benefit.

By the time we passed Jamaica, I'd given up the guessing game and sat looking idly out the window, wool gathering about Pa and the rest of us Bixbys and the screwy life we'd lived.

To begin with, Zebediah Bixby, which is Pa, was my entry for the catch-as-catch-can tipplership of the world. He should have been dead years before. A man who drank as much as he did just couldn't live long, yet there he was headed toward seventy and still going strong, guzzling away as he'd always done, and a lot healthier than my brother Cal, who has flat feet and asthma. I'm no sarsaparilla boy, but my venerable father can always drink me under the table.

Pa's one blind spot was Gibbon. Long before any of us were born, he got the idea he was going to re-edit Gibbon, but he never got any further than making bales of notes that always got lost or burned or held by landladies in the years he spent wandering in the cockeyedest corners of the world. He herded sheep in Australia, tended bar in Aberdeen, hunted gold in Alaska and fought a few revolutions in Central America, but mostly he was a newspaperman of the pre-Munsey *Sun* breed. Whatever job he had, he never would admit even to himself that it wasn't just a stop gap until he got his edition of Gibbon ready for the waiting world.

Pa married twice, and I guess his wives grew to hate the Roman empire. I know his kids did. He named us all for Roman rulers. Messalina was the first, born fifty years ago in Shreveport, Louisiana, between trains. Three years later, Caligula was born in San Luis Potosi, which is in Mexico. Then, when they were in Munich, Pa's wife ran away with a Greek guide from the waxworks museum. Pa once told me it was the guide's curly moustache, but I always had a private suspicion it was a case of too much Gibbon.

Pa's second wife had three children, but I was the

only one who lived. She died when I was born thirty years ago during one of Pa's intervals at the Bixby homestead at Scraffton Station. Pa named me Tiberius, dumped me on Messalina and Cal to raise and wandered down to New Orleans to take a job on the *Times-Picayune*. Messalina and Cal never felt I was a half-brother, and I didn't, either, but they never could get used to me. They thought I had bats in the belfry from birth. Maybe I did. I was like Pa in a lot of ways. I found that out after he turned up one day when I was about fifteen and told us he had decided to retire. We never did know just where the money came from or how much it was. It had something to do with a four-day stud game in Tampico and a silver mine belonging to a gentleman who labored under the unhappy delusion that three queens were unbeatable.

I was just making up my mind to get the whole story out of Pa this time when the train jolted to a stop and I saw we were in Mineola. As we pulled out, I went to the front of the car to get a drink of water and saw that the girl was reading a big book. She didn't look up, but Fish Eye saw me trying to get a squint at the title and gave me a sour look. A moment after I returned to my seat, he got up and stepped across the aisle. His coat was twisted up in back over the butt of a pistol in his hip pocket. I wondered that nobody else in the car saw it, but none of them did. He sat down a moment beside the girl and then went back to his seat. He was scowling about something. I reflected it would be a pleasure to poke him in the nose, but you can't go around just hitting people for no reason, especially guys with a pistol on the hip.

I lit a cigarette and opened my newspaper. It rattled, and the fat fellow across the aisle woke up and looked at me accusingly. Then he glared at the man in front of me. He had his paper spread out, too, so Fatty couldn't make up his mind which of us had rattled the paper. He snorted at both of us and settled back in his seat, closing his eyes again.

I went to get another drink of water, but I still couldn't see the title of the girl's book. Fish Eye gave me the dirty Double-O, but I pretended not to notice. I thought that if I was with a girl as swell looking as that, I wouldn't be sap enough to ride across the aisle from her. I noticed as I sat down that the seats behind Fatty's and mine were empty. The rest of the people, about a dozen, were scattered up toward the front of the car. The only woman in the smoker now was the girl in the red calot.

The conductor came through and took my ticket from the holder. Scraffton Station was the next stop. I noticed that he took the girl's ticket and Fish Eye's, too.

Fish Eye got up and walked past me toward the rear of the car. I wanted to turn around and look after him, but I didn't. I pretended to be deeply interested in the view from the window, but I could have sworn he paused a moment beside my seat as though uncertain whether to say something to me.

The train was slowing down to swing around a sharp curve. That meant we were crossing the creek through Doran's woods. I'd swum there many a time. I saw the sand banks were still there, and I remembered one of our stunts was to see who could jump the farthest into the sand from the railroad embankment. The woods were still as thick as ever, but by watching closely, I could just glimpse the roof of our house beyond the trees. I felt kind of gushy. Damn it, I was going to get home more often than once a year.

The girl got up and started toward the back of the car. The fat fellow dropped his cigar and woke up. It rolled into the aisle and he got up to get it. He blocked the aisle, so the girl had to stop a second at my seat. She had the book in her arm, a finger curled inside to hold her place. I could see two letters of the title. They were *SI* ...

I looked up at her, and our eyes met. She had the bluest eyes I'd ever seen. In that moment, I saw sharp, sudden suspicious glint in her eyes. Then she walked on. Her look had said as plain as words that she was afraid I had discovered some secret of hers. But that was tommyrot, of course. Fish Eye must have told her I was trying to make a play for her and she didn't like it.

I glanced around. She was just going in to the women's lavatory. She passed back to her seat not more than ten or fifteen seconds later. She didn't sit down, though. She stood there, dead white.

The train was stopping. I stood up. The conductor opened the door to the platform. Then the girl spoke.

"There's a man in the ladies' room," she said. "I think his throat's cut."

Chapter Two

The train was jolting to a stop as we gawked at her. Then we all started for the ladies' room at the same moment. The conductor opened the lavatory door, and we crowded behind him, all except the girl. She didn't budge. She looked as though she was going to faint.

A man was there, all right. He was doubled up under the wash basin as though somebody had shoved him under it. His head was still on, but it wasn't because somebody hadn't tried to take it off. A knife, or maybe a razor, had been dug in under his left ear and dragged forward. The blood bubbled, so I guessed he wasn't dead yet.

The conductor said, "He's alive. Get him out."

There was a great spout of blood when we moved him, and some of it got on the conductor's uniform. The man was dead when we laid him in the aisle. Fatty said, "Godamighty."

"Don't anybody leave," the conductor said. He stepped out into the vestibule and closed the door behind him. He kept his hand on the knob and called to somebody. Then I noticed the dead man's face. There wasn't any mistaking that mug. It was Fish Eye.

I turned quickly and looked at the girl. She was still standing beside her seat. Her eyes were wide and terror was in them. I couldn't think of anything to say, so I said, "I'm afraid he's dead."

"I'll say he is!" It was Fatty. He kept looking at the dead man's face as though he couldn't move his eyes. He said, "Godamighty." He sounded awed. The others were standing there goggle-eyed. The man who had been reading a newspaper in front of me spoke. He was a wispish little man with spectacles and a worried look. His voice was thin, querulous.

"They won't keep us here, will they?"

"I guess they will," I said. "It's a murder."

"I'll be late for luncheon and my wife will be worried sick."

Fatty said, "Godamighty." He was dazed, as though somebody had socked him on the head with a baseball bat. He said, "I think I'll sit down." He stepped back to his seat and sagged into it. He took a cigar out of his pocket, but didn't light it. He let it hang loosely in his pudgy fingers as though he'd forgotten it. I couldn't remember afterwards what the other passengers said or did.

The conductor came back with a brakeman and the stationmaster. He said, "I'll have to ask you to wait until the police get here." He pulled out his watch, breathed a sigh over his sacred schedule being shot to hell, and then put his handkerchief over the dead man's face. We all felt better after that.

The beetle of a stationmaster observed cheerfully, "Somebody sure did him up brown." Nobody answered him.

The little guy said, "My wife will be worried sick. Really, conductor; there's no reason for the train to wait here. Can't you take him off and go on? We're due at Clinton at 2:40 and we'll never get there with this delay."

"Sorry, but we've got to wait for the police. Nobody leaves this train until they get here. You had better take your seats to be sure nothing is disturbed."

The little man moved up to the front of the car as far away from the corpse as he could get and sat down fuming, tapping the windowsill with fretful fingers. The girl was still standing, and I walked up the aisle to her.

"You'd better sit down," I said. "We may have quite a wait."

She jumped as though I'd stuck her with a pin. She sat down. I sat down beside her, but she didn't seem to notice. She was holding her book in her lap, but I couldn't see the title. I fished out a pack of cigarettes.

"Smoke?"

She didn't turn around. She shook her head and kept looking out the window.

"Better change your mind," I said. "A smoke'll steady your nerves."

She didn't seem to hear, so I lit a cigarette. I took a deep drag and said, "I've got an idea you're going to need steady nerves when the cops get here."

She whirled. Her eyes were murder cold. There was fear in them, but more anger than fear. Her voice was low, taut.

"Meaning?"

"These county cops aren't dummies," I said. "They're going to wonder what you can tell them about your boyfriend's demise. They may even expect you to tell them why he picked the ladies' room to die in. That's a hell of a place to pick to get your throat cut, if you ask me."

"I'm not asking you."

"Okay. It's not my throat."

"I don't know what your game is, but you seem to have the idea that I knew … that man."

"Come off it, sister. I don't know why you two were pretending you didn't know each other, but I saw you before you got on the train. I saw him talk to you on the train, for that matter."

"I tell you …"

"Don't tell me. Save it for the cops. They might want to know who *he* was and what he had to bring."

She took it on the chin and didn't blink. "I don't remember inviting you to sit down here," she said.

"I know murder's hardly a social introduction, but I'm only trying to do you a favor."

"Aren't you rather large to be a Boy Scout?"

"Okay, Mrs. Astor."

I got up. I started to remind her that she must have seen the dying man the moment she opened the lavatory door. Yet she had gone inside and closed the door behind her. I started to ask her what she'd done there in those few seconds. I started to ask her why she hadn't said anything when she first came out. But a crazy impulse checked me. All I said was, "You'd better think up a story and, baby, it better be good."

The girl had guts, all right. She was scared stiff, but she wasn't yelling calf rope. Maybe that was why I played the sap when the cops arrived. A big dick named Rafe Conner was in charge, a red-faced Mick who looked like a cartoon of all the dumb flatfeet you've ever seen until you got a squint at his eyes. They were grey and cold and mighty seldom missed a trick. I'd known him since we were kids. He'd always liked me, probably because he beat me every time we'd had a fight. We hadn't seen each other in years, but he acted as though we saw each other every day. He never seemed surprised about anything.

The conductor told him, "Nobody's left the train. I thought you'd want to see them."

"That's fine," Rafe Conner said. He turned to a couple of the detectives who were with him. "Take the other cars. I'll handle this end myself."

He got a fill in from the conductor while the doctor fiddled around the stiff and then he poked his head into the lavatory. He went out to the vestibule and said something to a harness bull who was standing there, and the guy got off the train and started walking toward the rear cars. Another cop was beside the train, watching to see that nobody got off, and the other side of the train was covered, too. Conner stuck a couple of pieces of chewing gum into his face and munched them contentedly as he watched Evans, the fingerprint man, and his photographer go to work on Fish Eye. Then he glanced at his stenographer and started with the girl.

"I believe you found the body, Miss ...?"

"Jones," she said, "Gretchen Jones."

She said she lived on Commerce Street in New York, and I made a mental note of the number.

"Tell me just what happened," Rafe said.

"I ... well, I just opened the door and there he was," she said.

"Weren't you surprised to find a man with his throat cut?"

Her left eyebrow went up sharply. "Naturally," she said, and then she smiled nervously. "Oh, I see what you mean. I didn't scream or anything. I don't know why. It must have been the shock. I'm afraid it sounds stupid, but I didn't think of anything to do until I was back at my seat and then I told them."

"Did you know this man?"

"I never saw him in my life," she said. She seemed surprised at her own vehemence. "I don't mean to be so melodramatic about it, but I never saw a ... dead man before."

Rafe Conner seemed to be mulling something over and then he nodded to the man who was sitting behind her.

The girl asked, "Is ... is that all?"

"I'll have to ask you to wait until I finish with the others," the detective said. "Just a matter of routine."

The girl turned to the window and seemed to pay no attention to what the other passengers said. Not that they were any help. Some of them had noticed Fish Eye just as they would notice any other passenger, but that was all. None of them remembered seeing him leave his seat except the man sitting behind Gretchen Jones, and he couldn't remember just how long it was before the body was found.

"Did you see him speak to anybody? I mean, since you left New York."

I saw the girl's shoulders tense, and then relax slowly

when the man said, "I didn't notice. My wife's going to have a baby, and I was thinking about that pretty much. You know how it is."

The jittery little guy who was worried because he'd be late for lunch turned out to be Morley Smythe, head bookkeeper of the silk importing firm of Hepplewite & Cohen.

"I suppose," he said doubtfully, "I should tell you I have a small interest in the company, but that's supposed to be a secret."

"It won't go any further," Conner said. Mr. Smythe looked relieved.

"I know it's strange a business man should be coming home for luncheon on Monday, especially so long past lunch time," he said, "but, you see, I work all day Saturdays and all the others take a half day off, so I take my half day on Monday, and this is Monday, and so, you see, it is perfectly natural, after all, that I should be coming home to luncheon, a late luncheon, I mean, isn't it?"

"Perfectly," said Conner, and I marveled at his ability to keep looking at Mr. Smythe without laughing. God knows, I couldn't. I had to look out the window. Once I turned and saw the girl looking at me. I grinned, and she managed a smile. It was pretty sickly, though, and her eyes were questioning, fearful. Rafe Conner was saying, "Now about the murder, Mr. Smythe. Did you know the deceased?"

"Oh, good gracious, no! I never saw him before."

"Did you notice how he acted? Did he …"

"I didn't notice him at all. I'm afraid I never notice things. My wife says I never do. I'm sure I never saw him before … before they found him."

"I see. Well, did you notice what anybody else did? Say, Mr. Bixby here?"

Conner nodded toward me, and the girl glanced at me sharply. Mr. Smythe studied me a moment apprehensively before he replied.

"I did notice Mister ... er ... Bixby when I got on the train. I noticed he was sitting in the seat behind me, but that was all. You see, I was reading my newspapers. I read them very thoroughly, you know, and I'm afraid I was completely engrossed. I read the *Herald* on the train coming to town in the morning. I find it gives me vim for the entire day, especially Mr. Sullivan. He has such an incisive style, you know. Returning home, I read that morning's *Times* and the *Sun*. Of course, I do not read them as carefully, but I do read them. I believe we should know all shades of opinion before making up our minds on matters that confront the nation in these critical times, and so I read the *Times* and *Sun* as well as the *Herald*. I told my wife only the other day ..."

Next to bat was Fatty, who still seemed groggy as he identified himself as Herman Busch, a carpenter. He said he'd gone to New York to see his nephew about a cottage his nephew wanted built at Patchogue.

"God knows I don't know nothing about this here business," he said. "Sure, I guess I noticed him, but I don't know. I had a pretty hard day yesterday and I ain't had much sleep, and most of the time coming out I was asleep. I guess I ain't much help."

Rafe Conner patiently prodded and questioned and tried to wring a drop or so of information from him as he'd tried with all the others, but it was a washout. The best Mr. Busch could contribute was:

"Ain't it a terrible thing to happen? It might've been any of us."

"Not if you didn't go to the ladies' room," Conner said.

The detectives who'd gone through the rest of the train found out less than Rafe Conner did. Nobody had noticed anything or anybody suspicious. Plenty of passengers had passed through the cars for one reason or another, but nobody had noticed them especially. Most of them volunteered the information that they had left their car, some even saying they had gone up to the smoker, but there was nothing to indicate that any of these had sliced Fish Eye's throat and then gone back to their seat.

"Any of 'em could have done it," Conner observed, but that didn't seem to clarify matters much.

Evans and the photographer finished with the corpse, finished with the lavatory, and the dead man was lugged off in a wicker basket.

"Well," Conner said, "I guess that's that."

"I just know my wife will be worried sick," said Mr. Smythe.

"Ain't it terrible," said Mr. Busch.

The girl stood up. She was still holding the book so I couldn't see the title. I was trying to think what title began with *SI* when Rafe spoke to her.

"The conductor tells me you get off here," he said. "There are a few more things I want to clear up, but I can talk to you and Mr. Bixby at the station. There's no use holding the train any longer."

"Station?" she exclaimed.

"Railroad station," he said, stuffing another stick of gum into his mouth, studying her with expressionless eyes.

We trooped off the train. The passengers for Scraffton Station were leaving the other cars, too. The depot loafers were gawking at us, at the car behind us, but the girl didn't glance at them. She looked straight ahead as she walked to the waiting room with Rafe

Conner and the stenographer and me at her heels. Inside, she sat down and lit a cigarette.

"This is just routine," Conner said. His voice was soothing. "Just to complete the record, what's your business, Miss Jones?"

"A little of everything, I'm afraid. The last job I had was dancing in the chorus in a night club, the Golden Mirror. It's in Greenwich Village. That blew up a couple of months ago. Before that, I had a couple of other club jobs, did typing and for a week I was a receptionist at the Circle Broadcasting System. I must have lacked that winning personality, though, because they broadcast me right out of my job."

She smiled, and Rafe smiled back at her as though this was just killing time, and then he asked her why she was coming to Scraffton Station. She hesitated a moment and then she smiled again as though amused at something silly she'd done.

"I hope you won't laugh," she said. "It's really not as crazy as it sounds. You know, the *New Yorker* runs pieces about old New York, about the Hudson River towns and all that. Well, I haven't been able to get another job, and my money's about gone, and so I decided to try my hand at some articles like that. I came out here to see if I couldn't find something at your historical society."

Her voice was cool and ripply, just as though she didn't know I was going to spill the beans about her and Fish Eye. Her assurance irritated me. It would be just what she deserved to get slapped into the can on suspicion of murder. I glanced at the bulletin board on the station wall and saw a big placard announcing a Fourth of July celebration. In red letters across the bottom was "Scraffton Historical Society." So that was where she got the idea. Quick on the pick-up, all right.

I wondered if Rafe had seen the placard, but I guessed he hadn't. It was behind him. He was asking her how she happened to pick Scraffton Station to write about.

"I just got a time table and ran my finger down the list of towns until I came to one I'd never heard of," she said. "It seemed to me the best way to find one nobody else had written about. I hope it hasn't been written to death."

"I guess not," Rafe said. "Old man Pruitt can tell you, though. He's the head of the historical society. He can tell you everything that ever happened here."

"That's awfully kind of you," she said, fumbling in her purse, dragging out a pencil and an envelope, jotting down the name.

"I wouldn't let the Chamber of Commerce know how you found out about Scraffton Station," he said. "They're touchy about their municipal fame."

"I'll be discreet," she said.

She should have thought of that before she told that cock-and-bull story because I ...

"What do you know about all this, Tie?"

Rafe was looking at me, munching his gum. Gretchen Jones was standing by the door, pretending to be busy with her compact and her nose, but I knew she was waiting for my answer as a prisoner waits for the jury's foreman to answer.

I'm damned if I know why I lied. The instant I did, I wished I hadn't, but it was too late then. There was a fat chance Conner would believe me if I'd changed signals and said I'd just lied accidentally. I had to play the cards as I'd dealt them.

"I didn't notice him until just before we pulled in," I said. "Maybe five minutes before, maybe less. He went past my seat, back toward the ladies' room, but I didn't think anything of it. I was thinking of something else,

I guess."

"Why'd you notice him especially then?"

"Why? Search me. He just went past when I was looking, I guess. Who was he, anyhow?"

"Nothing in his pockets to show," Rafe said. He swallowed his gum as he got up. I remembered him swallowing his gum as a kid. He said, "You needn't wait any longer, Miss Jones. Thanks for helping us."

"I'm sorry I couldn't really help," she said. "I was wondering if you could tell me how to get to Mr. Pruitt's?"

"You'd better take a taxi. He lives out on Elm Road."

She looked helplessly around the taxi-less station, and I said, "I'm going that way. I'll show you the taxi stand."

"Give my best to your dad," Rafe said as we went out. The train had gone. The policeman Rafe had sent toward the rear of the train was far down the tracks, plodding toward us. Rafe went over to a couple of the other detectives who were waiting as the girl and I walked across the station square.

"You and the detective seem to be old friends," she said.

"Went to school together. This is my home town."

I was boiling at myself for having been such a sucker. There I was in the clear and I'd stuck my neck out for this dame I'd never laid eyes on before.

"I want to thank you," she said.

"Don't mention it."

We walked on a little way and I knew she was looking at me, but I wouldn't look at her. Finally she said, "If you dislike me so much, why did you do it?"

"I'm just a chronic liar. Can't tell the truth if my life depends on it."

"I'd have been in a bad hole if you hadn't come

through for me. Don't think I don't realize it."

"Why were you such a sap then? How'd you know I wouldn't tell him you knew the guy and dump over your little apple cart?"

"I didn't know," she said. "I might not have risked lying if I'd known at first you were the detective's friend, but … Oh, I'd have had to, anyway! I'd have had to gamble he'd believe me when I denied anything you told him. I couldn't let him know about …"

She broke off quickly. Her lips were pressed tightly together and she was looking straight ahead as we walked.

"Couldn't let him know about what?"

She didn't answer, and I said, "It seems to me I've got an explanation coming to me, even if the cops haven't."

"I can't tell you," she said. She stopped suddenly and looked at me. "Please believe me, I'm grateful for what you did. I'm sorry I was rude to you on the train. But I can't tell you anything."

"Well, I'm rude now, so that makes us even."

She tried a smile as we walked on. "Friends?"

"Hell, no. That guy's throat's not such a good recommendation for your friendship."

"Please, I …"

"Skip it, sister. You can get your cab across the street there at Joe's garage. I've got to get back to the station." The blue eyes narrowed suspiciously, but I said, "Don't worry, you know as well as I do that I've got to stick to my lie or get in hot water. Since I am in this, though, I want to find out what it's all about."

She put out her hand, but I ignored it. I said, "You'd better make good on your historical society gag. Conner's bound to check up on you."

"I don't blame you for being angry, but … you've got

to believe this. I didn't have anything to do with the murder."

"Sure, I know. Hitler didn't have anything to do with the war, either."

She flared at me. "Oh, you're acting like a fool!"

"Check, sister. I don't know why I lied to save your skin, but if ever I get the chance …"

"You won't," she snapped. She walked away across the street without giving me a chance for a comeback. I watched her talk to one of the fellows at the garage, and a moment later they drove off in a rattly sedan. I went back to the station. The cops were getting in their cars, and Rafe seemed surprised to see me.

"I thought you'd made a pretty swell pick-up," he said.

"I showed her the garage."

My mug must have showed I was mentally kicking myself around a dozen blocks, for Rafe said, "What's eating you, anyhow?"

"Nothing. I just feel lousy."

"Jump in and I'll give you a lift. The other boys are going to the station, but I've got to stop past home. Your place is on the way."

I got in with him, and we rolled off. I told him, "Say, there's something I forgot to tell you."

He chewed gum and looked straight ahead. I might be making a dopey play, but I wanted to open him up on the murder.

"I clean forgot it when you were talking to me, but that guy who got killed had a gun. I noticed it when his coat was caught up over it, but it must have slipped my mind."

"Say, you reporters are pretty blasé. A guy with a gat gets murdered under your nose, and you forget he was heeled."

"Just one of those crazy quirks of memory," I said. "And I'm not a reporter anymore. I'm a press agent. At least I was until the Little Flower's morality defenders put the slug on burlesque."

"He still had the gun. He never got a chance to pull it."

"That was a goofy place to pick for a murder," I said. "The killer was cutting it pretty thin just for space to swing his arms."

"Right, even if your pun is lousy. It wasn't a swing, though. It was a quick jab and a yank. Mister Man's jugular was sliced before he knew anything was wrong."

"I don't see how it was done without making a noise. He must have squawked, at least."

"Maybe he did, if the blood didn't strangle him before he could bleat. But the noise of the train drowned it. At least, it did unless some of you are lying."

"I still don't see how the guy …"

"Well, it was done. That's one thing we know. There've been a lot of murders that looked a lot more impossible to commit than this one."

"There ought to be fingerprints in the lavatory."

"But millions," he said.

"What about the prints of the people in the car?"

"We'll get 'em," Rafe replied. "You can't just grab a trainload of people and take their fingerprints. They'll calm down by the time we ask 'em to sign their statements and we'll get the prints. If we did it now, we'd have the whole shebang up in arms without doing us any good. Can you picture Mr. Morley Smythe if we'd asked for his fingerprints? The murderer probably wore gloves, anyhow."

"What did you make of the Jones girl?" I asked.

"Nice looking little piece. Why?"

"Nothing. I was just thinking of calling her in New York, maybe."

"Maybe."

Rafe said that except for the pistol, the dead man's pockets had contained only a couple of policy slips, a little over eight dollars in currency and change, a return trip ticket, three keys, two pencil stubs, a gold-plated watch with an empty locket charm and a torn sheet of paper on which a note was scribbled.

"I'll show you the note," he said as he swung the car to the curb in front of my house. "Maybe you can make something of it."

He fished it carefully out of his wallet. It had been torn raggedly from a notepad, the sort you find fastened in a lot of telephone booths to keep you from scrawling on the walls. It didn't seem to mean much. Some of the words trailed off into indecipherable scribbling.

"I had a hunch those illegible letters after *smo* might be *ker*, Rafe said. "That would be smoker, and he was killed in the smoker, all right. But that *211* doesn't mean, anything to me. It's not the number of the train and it's not the time it was due anywhere along the line. It gets in here at 2:15."

"Maybe *lad* and *can* aren't the same word," I suggested.

"So what? We know he was killed in a can, but ..."

"He was killed in a ladies' can," I said.

"Maybe you've got something. Let's see now: it's something about the ladies' can of the smoker, which checks pat, but what do you make of the rest? That *211* and those stars and stuff?"

"I don't know about the number, but that other junk looks like doodling to me. Haven't you ever doodled when you were telephoning? And that secret symbol at the top and the cross of stars, isn't that the sort of stuff a man does when he's waiting for his number to answer. As for Nuts, that's pretty clearly merely editorial comment."

"What about the weather in Oshkosh, then?"

"I leave that to you, Sherlock."

"If you're right, part of this is doodling and the rest is a message he got over the phone," he said. "So all I've got to do is find out if you're right and then find out what the hell it means."

"Good hunting," I said. I started to get out of the car, but Rafe stopped me. He was peeling another stick of gum.

"We found the weapon," he said casually.

"What was it, a razor?"

"A knife. He flushed it down the toilet, and I sent one of the boys back down the track to hunt for it. I figured what he'd probably done."

"That was pretty smart."

Rafe said, "Just routine," which was his way of saying, "the laws of God." He fished the knife out of his pocket. It was wrapped in a handkerchief.

"Never mind about prints," he said. "Evans tried it, and there aren't any."

I unwrapped the knife. It wasn't more than three inches long, hilt and blade, and it was slightly curved and razor sharp. The water had washed off almost all the blood. An elephant's head was carved on one side of the black bone hilt.

"Funny sticker, isn't it?" Rafe said. "I've seen one like it somewhere, but I can't remember where. Evans said it's like a stockman's knife."

"It's a Gurkha knife," I said.

"Oh, yes?" He looked at me a moment, slowly masticating his eternal gum, and then he said, "From India, huh?"

"That's right. They come in sets of three. There's a big one, a thick-bladed knife that could whack off your arm. Up near the mouth of the big knife's sheath are sewn a couple of small sheaths for babies like this little fellow."

"Not the kind of knife just anybody's liable to have?"

"I guess not, but they're pretty popular as souvenirs. If you're after an angle on 'em, I'd call Lacey's in New York. They're bound to have a flock of them in stock, and they know more about arms than anybody else in the country."

"Lacey's, huh?"

"Francis Lacey. It's down on Broadway."

"That's an idea. A set like this would look pretty good in a fellow's den, wouldn't it? Maybe I'll get one."

I went inside then, stopping at the door to wave to Rafe Conner as he drove off. The door was on the day latch, as always, so I didn't ring. I went inside and hung up my hat. I could hear Messalina in the kitchen, but I didn't want to see her just now. Too damned much had happened. I wanted to talk to Pa. As I climbed the stair, I became sure of one thing, at least.

The library door was ajar as I went up, and Pa didn't hear me. I paused; feeling a sentimental warmth at the old man sprawled out in an easy chair with the inevitable Irish-and-water at his right hand. Pa would have snorted if he'd known I ever felt sentimental about him. He sat now as he always sat: slumped down in the old chair at the far end of a long table, his face in profile against the back windows, his eyes moodily fixed on the wall of books at the far end of the room, his long legs stretched out in front of him so far that only the heels touched the floor and his thin feet jutted almost straight up in the air. He was tall, over six feet, and I never was able to decide whether the stoop of his narrow shoulders made him seem shorter than he was or taller. His skin was yellowish with years, and his fingers were long and thin. His white hair was wispy, but thick enough so he'd never have to worry about a toupee, even if he'd been the type. He had a droopy moustache, a sort of Lafcadio Hearn moustache. His face wasn't wrinkled, but the skin was tight and yellowed and old. When I spoke, he turned his head, and I wondered how I could have forgotten his eyes: deep sunk eyes, shadowed by craggy brows. They were green and there were flecks of fire in them and dark depths where things were hidden that none of us knew.

He said, "Hello, son," and we shook hands. He didn't get up, and I handed him the package.

"Sorry I haven't got a birthday verse, but happy birthday," I said. "Hope I didn't disturb too fond memories of past exploits."

He snorted. "A man's lucky who can forget his past. The men we used to be were invariably so dumb that they'd bore the socks off the men we are. If they weren't, they'd have had more sense than to become the men we are."

He tore off the wrappings, which he tossed under the table. He set the bottles of John Jameson's on the table and eyed them with approval.

"I give you," he said, "my paternal blessing as a most dutiful son. These bottles seem fat enough for an adequate celebration of the prodigal's return. Crack'er open, son."

While I opened one of the bottles and poured the drinks, Pa complained that Cal had passed out after only a single morning of drinking. "He tried, but I fear he lacks the essential spark of a true drunkard," he said with a sigh of regret. I passed him a glass and lifted my own.

"Natal felicitations," I said, and took a hefty swig. I started to tell him he was looking fine and fit, but he stopped me.

"Let's spare each other the customary lies and inquiries, son. We're both obviously alive, so let's drink to that admirable coincidence and skip the tedious amenities."

So we did. I nursed my drinks along, watching with wonder the way the liquor poured down his ancient gullet. He was an alcoholic miracle, and that was all that could be said by way of explaining him. The mere fact that he was still alive, sitting there with a glass of whiskey and water in his hand, was a flat contradiction of all the laws of nature, physiology, medicine and morals. But there he sat, rambling contentedly away, while I tried vainly to get the conversation onto the murder of Fish Eye. I had the jitters over it, over what I'd found out, but I might as well have tried to stop a herd of elephants as Pa. He was blasting Messalina because she'd at last insisted on having a telephone installed.

"It's so damned characteristic of mankind," he said. "If we happen to live where there are no lions to eat us, we aren't satisfied until we import some."

"You don't have to answer a phone, do you?"

"But you always do answer it. Its ringing is as enticing as Bluebeard's forbidden door. And answering it's about as devastating to one's peace of mind as opening that door, too."

"Will you forget the phone and listen to me. That murderer ..."

He went blandly ahead, "Phones, planes, automobiles—all they have done is speed up life so that people no longer have time to live."

"Listen, Pa, I've got to tell you ..."

He grinned. "Why waste fresh tears over old griefs? There never was a time when man's stupidity didn't wreck every hope he ever had of a sane and satisfactory life. And worrying about the fools won't give them brains."

"You've got to listen to me, Pa. The murder on the train ..."

"Murder's dull," he said. "Don't waste your time on trivialities that concern only the murderer and the murderee. Have a drink and ..."

I blurted it then.

"Maybe you won't think it's so unimportant when I tell you this—the murderer's knife came from this house!"

Chapter Three

Pa sat very still after I dumped it in his lap. His eyes were shadowed by his heavy brows. He didn't seem tight at all now. His voice was strangely low.

"I think you'd better sit down, son, and tell me about it."

So I began with my first sight of Gretchen Jones' red calot in the passageway in New York and, prompted by Pa's quiet questions, I told everything that had happened just as I've recorded it.

"I should have tumbled right off to the knife," I said, "but I didn't remember it until I was coming up the stairs. The sight of all your swords and pistols hanging on the stair wall made me remember the set of Gurkha knives you had. I found the sheath, all right, and two of the knives were still in it, but the other was gone."

"Which isn't proof that it's the knife Rafe Conner showed you."

"There's no chance of doubt, Pa. I examined it too closely to make a mistake. The elephants' heads on the hilts aren't usual, for one thing. And every last detail of the carving on the murderer's knife is the same as on ours."

"How did it get on the train, then?"

"Good God, if I had an idea about it, don't you think I'd have told you?"

"Easy, son. Let's make haste slowly. Does Conner know where the knife came from?"

"No. At least, I don't think so. He said he'd seen one like it somewhere, but he couldn't remember where. That's what I'm afraid of, he's liable to remember. When we were kids, we played with those knives dozens of times."

"I rather suspect your friend Conner does remember," Pa said. "Of course, we can't be sure, but he must know that a knife found on a railroad track isn't clinching evidence. A good defense lawyer could explain it away in jig time. Why wouldn't Conner, if he's smart, pretend he didn't remember the knife and try to get you into a panic by showing it to you?"

"That's screwy, Pa. What earthly reason ..."

"Simply on the gamble that you might lose your head and try to cover up more deeply. If you did, the chances are that you would reveal a great deal you'd already hidden securely. That is, if you were the murderer, of course. You aren't, are you, Tie?"

"Damn it, Pa …"

"Whoa, son! Don't snap the traces. If you're right about that knife, somebody took it out of this house. It might have been Messalina, or Cal, or me. You haven't been here in a year, but you could have taken it then. The rest of us weren't on the train, so we couldn't be the actual murderers. Still, we could have passed the knife to you or whoever the murderer was. Of course, the knife could be taken by anybody who came to the house, say by one of Messalina's D.A.R. sisters who cluttered up the house with a meeting a couple of weeks ago. The question is, why did whoever took that knife take that particular knife?"

"Oh, Pa, lay off being Socratic, can't you. If I knew the answers, I wouldn't be asking you."

"Somebody's brought us into this, and the only way we can protect ourselves is to find out who did it and why," he said, reaching for the bottle. "Do you remember that note well enough to reproduce it?"

"I think so," I said. I pulled out the table drawer and got a sheet of paper. I tore it to the size of the scrap found in Fish Eye's pocket as nearly as I could. I didn't remember everything right off, and I was a little doubtful about the exact number of stars, but finally I was satisfied that I'd made as good a copy as a man could without the original before him. I handed it to Pa and said, "Now you tell me."

He studied the scrap of paper carefully a few minutes and then put it in his pocket. He lit his pipe absently and took a sip from his glass. He had just turned to me to speak when Messalina came to the door to tell him dinner was ready. She made a great fuss over me.

As we talked, I noticed through the back windows that a light was lit in the Overhart house just across the alley fence from our backyard. I didn't care, but just to say something, I asked Messalina who'd rented it.

"It's not rented," she said. "Ruth's back. I thought I told you that the last time you were here."

"Maybe you did," I said. "What's she doing?"

"Why, Tiberius, you know very well she's a dentist."

"Oh, sure. But listen, sweet sister, you've forgotten something, too. Call me Little Annie Rooney or anything else you want, but don't call me Tiberius. It gives me the willies."

"I did forget, Tie. I'm sorry."

Pa broke in. "Don't let her get started on the great female dentist," he warned. "I've been hearing Dr. Ruth Overhart until I'm groggy."

"Now, father, you're unfair."

"Tall, lanky female with mouse colored hair. I never could abide the breed."

"Father, you mustn't. Ruth never was a pretty girl, but she's an admirable woman. She's made quite a success with her dentistry."

"Doesn't change my mind," he retorted. "She's the one who used to wheedle you to make Tie take her on hayrides, isn't she? Thought so. Well ..."

"Ruth has become a very smart looking woman," Messalina said, tossing her head defiantly.

"I can't see a woman dentist getting much practice in Scraffton," I said. "Didn't the Ladies Aid protest?"

"Ruth's done very well. She's very capable. She blossomed out after her parents died. I'm afraid they sort of held her down, poor thing."

She sailed out then, and as we followed her down to dinner, Pa spoke too softly for her to hear.

"Don't mention this to Messalina or Cal," he said. "Wait until we've worked something out and can see daylight."

Cal was still out cold upstairs, so there were only the three of us at dinner. Pa didn't say much, and I didn't feel like talking, either, but Messalina didn't notice. She kept up a rapid fire about people I'd known, people I'd forgotten and people I'd never met. She said the old Hope place next door to the Overhart home had been rented by a family named Wannerman.

"I don't know much about them, but they're nice, quiet neighbors," she said. "That white building you saw in the back of the house …"

"I didn't see any."

"Oh, you must have, Tie. A low white building near the fence, just cat-a-cornered across the alley?"

It was too much trouble to argue. "Maybe I did," I said.

"That's Mr. Wannerman's laboratory. He's some sort of scientist, but I don't know what he does exactly. I met him at Ruth's office when he was having a tooth filled. He seemed a nice man, though he didn't really say much, and he did say he suffered a lot with his teeth, and I suppose that …"

Pa looked up from his plate. He laid down his knife and fork and looked at his chattering daughter.

"Messalina," he said, "will you please stop trying to make conversation?"

"Why, father!"

She flushed to the roots of her hair, brown salted with grey and pulled straight back from her face to a tight knot at the back of her head.

"You're a sweet girl," he said, "and God knows you deserve a better family than you've got, but when you try to make conversation, you're as futile as a lion with a Christian to eat and no teeth."

Messalina smiled wanly and toyed with her food. I wondered why she didn't eat. Pa was silent a moment before he went on.

"Caligula was telling me about them," he said. "Man's a chemist with a silk formula. Says he's got some way to make silk out of wood fiber. Just needs perfecting for commercial production. Seems to have plenty of backing."

"Why," said Messalina, "I didn't even know Caligula knew him!"

"Says he doesn't. Says Nalor told him. Nalor's got a job as night watchman at the fellow's lab."

Messalina looked hurt that Caligula should have kept something from her. She said she guessed Nalor was lucky to get a job because his wife was going to have another baby.

"Nalor doesn't deserve a job," Pa said. "No man who keeps having children does."

"Father!"

Pa sank into silence, and neither Messalina nor I said much after that. When Pa is in a reflective mood, he doesn't like a lot of talking around him. He told me once that in such moods he forces himself to be introspective, though he detests introspection.

"Introspection," he announced, "is an intelligent man's Gethsemane. It's an essential step toward his crucifixion—and spiritual resurrection."

When we were going back to the library after dinner, Messalina said she'd telephoned Ruth Overhart to come over for a little while. I could have slapped her for it, but I didn't say anything. I looked at Pa and he grinned.

"I might as well warn you," he said, "Messalina has picked Ruth out to be your bride. You'd just as well give in and propose."

"Why, father!"

When Ruth did turn up, I was glad to see her because it interrupted Pa in a dissertation on the Antonines. Messalina had stayed in the room, so we hadn't had a chance to discuss the murder, but I was damned if I wanted to hear about a gang of guys who were so honest they were ineffectual. Or rather, who were honest and, therefore, were ineffectual. You don't need to go back to Rome for examples of that. At least, not if you know your America.

Messalina had been right about Ruth. She'd improved a little since the days when, though I was six or seven years younger, she'd wangled me to take her on hayrides so she wouldn't have to stay home. She was tall, lithe, crisply tailored, but her hair was still mouse colored.

I heard a door bang somewhere out back and glanced out of the window. It was dark now, but I could see the blur of somebody in light clothes walking from the Wannerman house to the laboratory. A moment later, a light went on in the lab.

"Your friend Wannerman's working late," I said.

"You know Dirck?"

"Messalina was telling me about him."

"He's not a bad sort," Ruth said, "but he's too serious. He makes his poor wife miserable at times."

A car swung into the driveway of the Wannerman house and in the momentary glare of the headlights sweeping across the lawn, I thought I saw a dark figure running across the Wannerman's yard toward the lab. I heard the car door slam. The automobile lights went out. I strained my eyes at the point in the darkness where I'd seen the running figure, but I couldn't pick anything out of the darkness. I told myself not to be such a jittery sap; I'd be seeing green elephants next.

Somebody was calling out at the Wannerman's. It was a woman's voice. She was on the back porch. The light showed her to me as she leaned through the back door. I saw a shaft of light as the lab door opened. I couldn't hear what the woman said, but the man's voice replying from the lab was louder.

"Tell him to wait," he said. "I'll be in right away."

The lab door closed again. Ruth was talking to Pa. In this light, she was not such a bad looking dame. She'd been a good egg in the old days. I took her on hayrides, but when I needed a dollar or so to take a girl I was soft on to the movies, Ruth was always good for a touch. Now she was saying, "I wanted to wish you happy birthday, Mr. Bixby. I hope …"

Then it happened. There was a dull explosion. Before I could figure out what it was, there was a burst of flame from Wannerman's laboratory. Messalina stood up at the sound. At the sight of the flame, she screamed. She was dead white.

Ruth was first down the stairs. I stumbled over Messalina in the hall, so Ruth was across our backyard and out into the alley before I left the house. The last thing I heard in the house was Pa telling Messalina to stay where she was and not be a helpful idiot.

I tried to follow Ruth, but once I was in the alley, I couldn't find the gate in the high board fence that surrounded the Wannerman property. I could hear a woman screaming and men shouting, and the whole neighborhood was lighted up by the flames that roared upward from the building. Wannerman must have chemicals stored in the building for the fire to spread so fast. But he was bound to have chemicals. It was a laboratory, wasn't it?

I yelled to Ruth to tell me where the gate was, and then I felt like a damned fool. She couldn't hear me above all that bedlam. It wasn't a high fence, and I managed to pull myself up and drop over it. I landed on my bottom. It jarred me. My palms were scraped from the top of the fence. I cursed blue blazes.

I'd fallen over the fence at the far corner of the wide yard from the flaming laboratory. I could see about a dozen figures silhouetted against the fire. Two of them were holding a struggling woman. I guessed it was Mrs. Wannerman. She was trying to throw herself into the flames. She was yelling.

"He's there!" she screamed. "He's there! Oh, let me go!"

Wannerman must be inside, then. Poor devil. He was a goner now.

I started across the wide lawn. I had to pass through a sprawling, thick grove of high shrubs and evergreens that shut the group at the fire from my side. It was dark in the thicket and I stumbled. I cursed and bumped into something that hurt my shins. I turned to go back and tripped over something. The next instant I crashed into somebody.

"Hey, watch ..."

That's as far as I got. Something hard crashed against my head. It was like skyrockets in my eyes. I grabbed wildly in the dark. My left hand clutched a struggling figure. The next instant I howled from a kick on my shin. I went down. I grabbed crazily for something, and my fingers clutched a soft thing that came off in my grasp. I could hear my enemy sobbing. I tried to scramble up and fight, but I couldn't make it fast enough. I heard him running. I got up to pursue, but the sound of the fleeing feet had died away. There was no sign of the fugitive.

The woman at the fire was screaming, "They've killed him! They've killed him!"

I could hear the fire engines clanging toward us. I limped a few steps, stumbled out of the grove. I stopped to get my breath. I saw then by the light of the fire the soft thing I had snatched in the fight in the thicket. It was a red calot.

Chapter Four

The woman had stopped screaming and was sobbing in Ruth Overhart's arms when, after stuffing the red calot in my coat pocket, I went on to the group standing a little way apart from the burning laboratory. The firemen were running hose lines in, and Ruth was saying, "Come in the house, Emma. We can't do anything to help."

"No ... No ... Oh, they've killed him ... They've killed him ..."

"You've got to snap out of it. We don't know ..."

"They've killed him ... I know they have...."

It was Mrs. Wannerman. I couldn't see her face because it was buried against Ruth's shoulders, but her grey-streaked hair and the wide hips that looked even wider in the shapeless flower print dress gave me a pretty good idea that her face wouldn't be anything to launch even a skiff about. Her flabby body sagged in Ruth's strong arms. She kept moaning, mumbling, "They've killed him ... They've killed him ..."

Most of the others, neighbors in their shirtsleeves and gaping housewives, had already lost interest in Mrs. Wannerman and were craning their necks to see if they could spot the body through the windows of the burning lab. One of the men didn't seem interested in the fire, though. He kept darting covert, suspicious glances at the sobbing woman. His tongue flicked over his lips with a snaky motion. I didn't like his looks. He was too spick and span, and his suit was one of those flashy creations with padded shoulders and a wasp waist. His slick hair glistened with grease, and I could have won dough betting he used perfumed pomade. I wondered where he came from. He just wasn't the Scraffton Station type. A big lug with a dumb look went over to this rat-faced little guy and said something I couldn't hear. Rat Face snapped at him, flinging up a hand in annoyance, and the big guy went back out of the circle of firelight, but I caught the look in his eyes as he studied Rat Face. It was a cold look, a look of calculating suspicion. Or maybe, I told myself, I was just getting the heebies. Things were happening too fast for me. The murder on the train, the Gurkha knife, the girl in the red calot and now Rat Face suspicious of Mrs. Wannerman and the big guy suspicious of Rat Face and ... Oh, hell, I'd be cutting out paper dolls next.

Ruth was saying, "You've got to come inside, Emma. You can't stay here."

"No ... No ..."

Ruth's cool voice murmured comfortingly and she started slowly toward the house, half-leading, half-supporting the moaning woman. Ruth saw me and said, "Lend a hand, will you, Tie?" So I put an arm around Mrs. Wannerman and between us we got her to the house. Her feet were half-dragging as we led her inside, as we took her up the stairs, and she didn't seem to know what we were doing to her. Rat Face followed a few steps, but stopped. She never let up on the moaning:

"They've killed him ... They've killed him...."

"You mustn't, Emma. People will think ..."

"I know they have ... I told him ... I told him they'd kill him...."

When we got Mrs. Wannerman to her room, she sagged down on the bed, turning her face into the pillow, muffling her dry, moaning sobs. Ruth bustled into the bathroom and came back with a wet towel.

"Wait downstairs, Tie. I'll get her to bed."

"Sing out if I can do anything."

"I will, thanks."

I had reached the head of the stairs when Ruth came to the door of the room and called me back. She seemed worried about something.

"You'd better call her doctor," she said. "Dr. Thompson. I think you'll find ..."

"Sure, I know him."

She returned to Mrs. Wannerman. The woman was still moaning, "I told him ... I told him they'd kill him."

I went slowly downstairs, wondering who they were, wondering where the red calot fitted into this mess of lies and murder and fire and a burning corpse. There wasn't a phone in the hall, so I went on into the living room, a long room that ran the length of the house from front to back. The only light was the ruddy glow from the burning lab. The reddish light fell through the high French doors that opened onto a rear terrace overlooking the back lawn and the lab, and it was light enough for me to see a heavy Staffordshire lamp on a book-cluttered table. I pulled the lamp chain and blinked in the sudden light. I looked around, but I didn't see a phone. I was about to leave when out of nowhere came a voice.

"Turn off that god damned light!"

I didn't see anybody. The voice said, "Will you turn it

off, or do I have to smash it?"

I realized then that the voice, the husky voice of a woman, came from a big wing chair pulled up in front of the open French doors so she could watch the laboratory burn.

"Sorry," I said. "I was looking for a phone. Mrs. Wannerman needs a doctor."

"She needs a hell of a lot more than that. Only turn out that light! I hate light. I want ..."

"Sorry," I said and pulled the lamp chain. Again the room was dark except for the fire glow spilling through the terrace doors. The voice said, "If you've got to have a phone, it's on the desk."

"Thanks."

"Don't mention it. Don't mention anything. Just let me watch that damned ..."

Her voice trailed off, and I wondered at the hate in it as I went to the kneehole desk at the front of the room and found the telephone hidden behind stacks of books and magazines. I called Dr. Thompson and told him Ruth Overhart thought he ought to come over right away. Instead of leaving then, I strolled down to the other end of the room to where the woman was sitting. I wanted a look at this dame whose husky voice was so compelling, this daffy dame who hated light.

I said, "I'm sorry I ..."

"Skip it."

She didn't look up. She was slumped down in the big chair, her chin sunk on her chest, and she was staring fixedly through the open French door to where the black shapes of the crowd and the firemen could be seen gnomelike against the glare of the fire. She looked pretty drunk. I stood uncertainly silent, and then she spoke again without even glancing at me.

"Did they get him out?" she asked.

"I'm afraid not. I …"

"Damned good riddance." Her voice was brittle with hate. She lifted the highball glass she was holding to her lips and the fire glinted on her red-stained fingernails. The glass was empty and she frowned. She turned toward me then, and by the flickering light cast from the burning lab I got my first good look at her face. She was dead-white and her mouth was a carmined splash. Her hair was honey-colored, thick in tumbled waves. But what hit me hardest were her eyes. They were the eyes of a cat who has killed a bird.

She looked at me a moment and then seemed to realize for the first time that I was a stranger, and her eyes widened a little, questioning, but all she said was, "Fix a couple of drinks. I'm tired of bartending."

Scotch, soda and a bowl of ice cubes were on a copper tray on the table beside her chair, and I mixed a couple of drinks, trying to think of something to say, wondering who was this lush, lazing young woman in shimmery green, this woman who found pleasure in watching a man burn to death.

I gave her a drink and she took a deep swig. She said, "Sit down, since you're here." I sat down and sipped my drink, watching her as she turned back to look at the fire, and the light of the fire danced weirdly, drunkenly over her face and her hair. Finally she glanced at me again.

"You don't happen to have a fiddle, do you?" She squinted at me and said, "I guess you don't. You don't look like Nero." She took another gulp of her drink. "Where'd you come from, anyhow?"

"I'm from across the alley. I saw the fire and thought I might help."

"Just a Boy Scout doing his good deed." She laughed shortly. She was the second dame who'd called me a Boy Scout. "Well, I'm glad he didn't get out."

"You don't seem to like Mr. Wannerman."

"Why should I?" she said. "I'm his daughter."

There didn't seem to be anything to say to that, so I drank again and didn't say anything. She didn't notice it, though. She was rambling on, as much to herself as to me.

"That's me. Little Paula, the pride of the Wannermans. And I'm not so dumb. I could tell plenty. You're damned right I could if I wanted to. And wouldn't you like to know!"

"Not particularly."

"Oh, yes, you would. Everybody would. The whole damned world would like to know. But I'm not talking. Little Paula's not spilling anything, not even to her Boy Scout."

"It's okay by me, lady."

"You think you can act that way and I'll tell. Well, you got another think coming, Boy Scout. And I'll tell you why. I'm glad! That's why I'm not telling. I'm glad he's dead, the dirty bastard!"

Her voice shrilled. She suddenly flung her glass to the floor. The crash of the glass made me jump up and I stood staring stupidly at the pool of liquor spreading among the shattered glass. I might have been in China for all the attention she paid me. She was staring at the fire again.

"I guess I'll be going," I said.

"Sure, sure, go 'way. You're like all the rest. You're so damned …"

"Take it easy," I said, and she whirled on me. Her eyes were blazing drunkenly and her twisted mouth was suddenly ugly.

"You thought I didn't see! You think I don't know! You think I won't tell! God damn you, I'll ..."

She sprang up and rushed at me. She tried to claw my face, but I grabbed her wrists. She was panting.

"I'll kill you! I'll kill ..."

I flung her from me, and she sprawled on the couch. She tried to struggle up, but I pushed her back and held her shoulders. She wriggled and twisted, and I tightened my grip. Suddenly pain shot through my arm. She'd bitten my hand, the bitch. My hand whipped viciously across her face. Her head jerked back and she went limp. I released her and stood up. She didn't try to rise. She just lay there rumpled, tousled, and her eyes burned with hatred. I was straightening my tie when she spoke. Her voice was low, trembling.

"I'll kill you," she said. "I'll kill you if it's the last thing I ever do."

Before I could answer, a voice spoke behind me. "Don't be a fool, Paula!"

It was Ruth. Paula didn't look at her. She kept her eyes fixed on me. I walked over to the door.

"God, is she soused," I said. "Tried to claw my eyes out."

"Don't pay any attention to her," Ruth said.

"I'll pay enough attention to break her damned head if she tries anything."

"You mustn't think anything of ... anything she may have said." Ruth's voice was low so the girl couldn't hear. "She's a psychopathic case when she's drinking."

"She's something, all right."

Ruth bit her lip, hesitated. Then she said, "Please find out what's happening outside, Tie. I'll attend to her."

I had a sudden suspicion that for some reason Ruth

Overhart wanted to get me out of the house; that for some reason she wanted me where I couldn't talk to Paula Wannerman. Then, as the door slammed behind me and I started across the lawn, I told myself I was getting screwy. I'd be suspecting I killed Fish Eye next. But, damn it, who did? What the hell was Gretchen Jones doing running away from the fire? What could the drunken blonde tell if she would? And why did she hate her father so much she was glad he was dead?

The firemen had controlled the blaze. Only the far corner of the building was still burning, and the firemen were wetting down the blackened walls. They had set up a couple of big searchlights, and I went over to Chief Rainey. He was talking to the ambulance surgeon from the county hospital. He was saying, "We never would've got it if Nalor hadn't happened to come back."

We shook hands, and I asked about Mrs. Rainey, and he said she was getting on fine.

"Wannerman's in there?" I asked.

"Yeah. We could see him, but couldn't get to him. The boys'll be able to get the body out pretty soon."

"What's this about Nalor."

"He's Wannerman's watchman at the lab and would've been here tonight, but Wannerman said he was going to work all night and Nalor could have the night off. Nalor forgot his raincoat and came back to get it. He happened to get here just as something exploded inside. He tried to get in to get Wannerman, but it was burning too fast already, so he ran to the house and called us."

"To late to do Wannerman any good."

"Yeah, too late. Want to see him?"

I followed him closer to the smoldering ruin and we

looked through a gaping, charred window. He pointed to a blackened mass in the middle of the long laboratory, switching his flashlight on it, and I saw the shapeless, huddled figure of a man crumpled against a low cabinet as though he'd tried to hide from the fire.

"Must have caught him while he was working," Rainey said.

He called to a couple of the firemen, and we went inside with them, picking our way through the tangle of charred timbers. Wisps of smoke still rose from the debris at our feet. I asked the chief what caused it, and he shrugged.

"Gas, I guess. Or maybe he mixed the wrong things. He was some sort of chemist."

I heard somebody crunching behind us and looked back. Rat Face was following us, and I nudged the chief. Rainey told him he'd have to wait outside.

"I'm Mr. Wannerman's attorney. I ..."

"You'll have to wait outside just the same, mister."

Rat Face scowled, but he left. I remembered a fire when I was a kid and Pa was working on the *Chronicle* down in Houston, Texas. Some of the bodies came apart when they were lifted, but this one didn't. It was just a hunk of charred filth, blackened and raw-red, burned out of human semblance but the firemen had kept water playing on it, and so the widow would have enough to bury, anyhow.

When they lifted the dead man into a blanket and carried him out, I noticed a patch on the right side of his face wasn't burned. When he fell, that portion of his face had been pressed against the cupboard and so had escaped the flames. The cupboard was burned black except where his face had rested, and that blistered patch of varnish was streaked with white, and I could see the outline of his ear printed in white in the melted varnish. I remembered the Webster Avenue fire in Houston. That was after Pa got me a job on the *Press*. A woman named Raab and a man were burned in a house, a torch job, and the woman had fallen against a sideboard. Her ear had been printed in the sideboard varnish like this, only her whole ear had showed, and on the cupboard here I could see only the thick, full lobe and the wavery upward line. It was lucky I got interested in the print of the dead man's ear or I'd have missed what I saw then. It was something the others had overlooked, and even so, I wouldn't have noticed it if one of the searchlights hadn't been fixed so it streamed through a window onto the cupboard. What I noticed were wide-headed thumbtacks driven into the side of the cupboard, close together, like the pips of a playing card.

The dead man's face had kept the tack heads from being burned over by the flames. I took out my pocketknife and scraped at the charred surface of the side of the cabinet. I found it studded with dozens of thumbtacks. Right then I'd have bet my shirt I knew the answer to the fire.

My task was made more difficult by the necessity of bending over from one side of the cabinet so that my body wouldn't shut off the searchlight by which I worked. Then, gingerly, as carefully as a surgeon opening a belly, I used the smallest, thinnest blade of my penknife to pry out a bunch of the tacks. I didn't find what I was looking for under most of them, but the heads of the five tacks which had been protected by the face of the corpse and a few others hid tiny black discs just the size of the tack heads. It was another break for me. Whoever had stuck all those tacks in the cabinet had been so nervous he—or she—had pressed the heads of some of them so tightly against the wood that the fire couldn't reach the discs underneath. I took an old please remit letter out of my pocket and dropped the little black discs into the envelope. Chief Rainey called me from the door.

"What're you doing, Tie? You better get a move on."

"Coming," I said. I tried to make my voice sound casual so Rat Face or his hulking pal or—well, anybody else outside wouldn't tumble that I'd found anything. When I got outside, I buttonholed the chief and got him out of earshot of the others.

"I've got something, chief. This is a torch job."

His eyes narrowed, but he didn't crack. I gave him the envelope and told him where I'd got the tiny discs it contained. He glanced inside and then slipped the envelope into his pocket to wait until he was where there was more light, and he looked sharply at me.

"I'll bet my shirt you'll find those discs are movie film," I said. I told him how I'd happened to find the tacks and how I'd found the discs under some of the tack heads. I didn't have to draw him a blueprint, for Chief Rainey knew as well as I did the old arson stunt of stringing movie film so fire will spread swiftly through a building when it's touched off. If this wasn't a touch-off, why was an expensive laboratory cabinet stuck full of thumbtacks? We'd never have noticed the tacks or the film if the dead man's face hadn't protected those five tacks, and even then I wouldn't have noticed them if I hadn't been looking at the print of his ear and been remembering the Raab case.

"I'll bet that damned place is as full of tacks as a hardware store," I said. "I don't envy you guys the job of finding 'em, though."

"I'm calling the D.A. There's a phone at the house,

ain't there?"

"In the living room. I'll go along ..."

Rat Face came sidling over to us with a smirk on his greasy pan, and I saw the big guy edging over, too, keeping an eye on the gaudy little lawyer.

"What's up, chief?" I guess Rat Face thought he was using a hearty voice. "Find anything important?"

The chief didn't answer, and Rat Face pulled out an alligator hide wallet and took a card, which he presented to the chief with a flourish.

"That's me," he said. "Salvatore Fiore. Sally Fiore. I guess you've heard of me."

"Can't say I have." The chief dropped the card in his pocket without any indication that he cared whether he ever heard of Mr. Fiore or not. "I'm sort of busy now," he said.

"Listen, chief, you don't want to do nothing you'll be sorry for. This mug brought something out of that house in an envelope, and I want to know what it is. I got a right to know. It's the law. I'm Wannerman's lawyer and I got to protect his interest. I ..."

"He's dead."

"Well, the widow's interest. Same thing. I'd advise you ..."

"I don't need no advice, mister. But I'll give you some. Just save your breath until the cops get here. They'll want to hear a lot about Mr. Wannerman."

"Cops? Whatta y'mean, cops?"

"You better wait and ask them," Rainey said. He went on toward the house. I trailed along, and Mr. Sally Fiore went hop-skippety-jump at the chief's other elbow. I glanced over my shoulder and saw the lug tailing us with his hat pulled down so it was hard to get a good look at his face, not that anybody would have wanted to look at his pan for pleasure.

"I demand an explanation, chief." Mr. Fiore obviously had the jitters. "I am attorney for the deceased, and anything ..."

"You'll have to wait, mister."

Fiore darted a look at me. "Who's this young man?" he demanded. "By what authority does he go searching that place when the owner's attorney is refused permission to ..."

"Mr. Bixby," said the chief, "meet Mister ... I didn't just get the name."

"Fiore, Salvatore Fiore. I want to know ..."

"Mr. Bixby sort of helps me out on difficult fires," Chief Rainey said as smooth as smooth, but if I'd been Mr. Sally Fiore, I'd have taken warning from the tightening at the corners of the chief's mouth.

As we went inside, Fiore took my arm and tried to get confidential. I knew who he was, all right. I guess most of New York knew Sally Fiore. He was Nicky Pet's mouthpiece. He'd made his name as counsel for big shot bootleggers back in prohibition days, and there were plenty of ugly tales that Sally Fiore was a lot deeper in his clients' dirty work than merely their legal adviser. Nobody'd ever been able to hang anything on him, though.

Fiore was saying, "It'll save a lot of time, young man, and I'll see you don't regret it if you'll just tell me ..."

"I've got all the time in the world," I said. "You'll have to ask the chief."

Rainey was half a dozen steps ahead of us down the hall. Fiore lowered his voice and tightened his grip on my arm. "Listen, sap, if you want to stay healthy ..."

I jerked my arm free. I knew I was being a damned fool, but I was too sore to care.

"Listen yourself, squirt! Get the hell out of here before I smear you."

"You don't know who I am, huh?"

"You may be a little tin Jesus to Nicky Pet, but to me you're just the reason we have a sewer system."

"I'll make you ..."

"Will you walk out, shyster, or will I throw you out?"

I took a step toward him, and he scuttered off out the hall door. I saw the big guy was waiting for him. I stalked down the hall to the living room. Later, when I cooled off and thought about what I'd done, I got so scared I had the shakes, but at the time I was too mad to be frightened.

The chief was already telephoning when I entered the living room. Ruth and Paula Wannerman were sitting on the couch, neither looking at the other. For my money, they'd been having a row. Both of them were white around the lips, and Ruth's hands were clinched in her lap. I went over to her.

"Could I see you a second, Ruth? It's important."

She didn't have a chance to answer. Paula turned on us. If looks could kill, we'd both have dropped in our tracks.

"What is there I can't know? It's my father that's dead, isn't it? I've got a right to know."

My greatest desire at that moment was to smash my fist into somebody's face. Just anybody's.

"I thought you were giving loud cheers he was dead," I said.

"What if I was? I'm still his daughter. If you've got anything to say, say it."

"Okay, sister. You asked for it. The fire's a touch-off. Arson. The chief's calling the D.A. now."

The blonde hussy hadn't budged. She'd taken my arson crack without so much as lifting an eyebrow. Now she was leaning back on the couch, watching me from under half-closed lids.

She made a lazy gesture toward a cabinet. "You might make a drink," she said. Her voice was a purr. "You ought to be nicer to me, Boy Scout. Someday you're going to be sorry."

I let it slide. After all, you can't very well tell a woman you think she's a rainbow-colored bitch when you're drinking her liquor. Not even a screwy dame like Paula Wannerman.

"You might ask me to have one, too," she said.

"Okay. Have one?"

"A strong one. Scotch. I've got sorrows that need drowning."

I couldn't resist the chance. "Sort of belated, aren't they?"

I'd expected her to flare up, but she didn't. She just snuggled lower into the cushions and her voice was silken. She wasn't looking at me when she answered. She was covertly watching Ruth Overhart. Ruth didn't know it, though. She sat bolt upright, her hands in her lap, looking straight ahead. The blonde was saying, "Papa's no worry of mine. The only favor he ever did me was dying. But there're others who can't …"

Ruth stood suddenly and walked out of the room without looking at us. I had her drink in my hand, so I drank it. I sat down on the couch.

"What's wrong with Dr. Overhart? You'd think it was her father that …"

"Hardly her father."

"If you mean what I think you do, you're a screwball. She's not the type."

She frowned with sudden annoyance. "Oh, run away and get your scoutmaster to tell you about the bees and flowers!"

"If you're smart, you'll stop spouting cracks like that about Dr. Overhart."

"Oh, all right, Sir Pure-of-Heart. I didn't mean she was his mistress, anyhow. She's nuts about him, but it never did her any good."

"I suppose she told you that?"

"Not at all. I'm not in her confidence and, please God, I'll never be. But a girl has eyes to see with."

She leaned forward and put her hand on my knee. She didn't say anything for a moment; just looked at me. "Listen," she said at last, "and don't think I'm clowning. You're in this already, I know, but don't butt in any deeper if you want to stay in one piece. I don't know what it's all about, but I know you're playing with dynamite."

"Thanks for the sudden solicitude."

She stood up and said, "It's nothing to kid about. I'm over my head, and you know some of the answers, but you don't know them all. I don't know what angle you're playing and I don't care. But if you keep poking your nose into other people's business, you're going to wake up some morning and find it cut off."

Something about the green eyes kept me from cracking wise. I finished my drink and got up as she walked toward the door.

"Couldn't I offer you another drink of your liquor?"

"No, thanks," she said. "I think I'll go upstairs before the place is cluttered with cops."

"Just one thing before you go. Would you mind telling me on the level why the interest in my welfare?"

"Maybe I'm just plastered enough to like you," she said.

She was swaying a little. I tried another tack. I got confidential and said, "Everybody's talking riddles, Miss Wannerman, and I want to know what it's all about."

"If you don't know already, you'll never know."

"I'm pretty good at crossword puzzles."

"If you keep on, you're liable to wind up being an eight-letter word meaning Boy Scouts shouldn't be so nosey."

She took a step toward me. The lazy languidness was gone. Her voice was low, tense. Her eyes were the deepest green I ever saw.

"Be smart, Boy Scout. You're way over your head. Get back in shallow water before you drown."

"Don't worry about me. I'm Leander in disguise."

She went hoity again. "Oh, well, if you think you can outswim a man-eating shark, it's your funeral."

"Getting back to your eight-letter word," I said. "Would it by any chance be 'defeated'?"

She stood a moment silent, swaying. The green eyes burned. Her voice was brittle.

"No," she said. "Murdered."

Chapter Five

Paula Wannerman walked quickly out of the room before I could open my mouth. She left me flabbergasted, bogged down in questions I couldn't answer. I lit a cigarette and tried to think some sense into the jumble; tried to figure out who the blonde had meant would kill me for butting in. The question that kept prodding me most was where the red calot, crumpled in my pocket now, fitted into this mess of murder and death by fire.

The doorbell rang. The servant let in Rafe Conner and another county dick, a red-faced guy named Bellows. Conner lifted an eyebrow at seeing me, but all he said was, "You sure do get around, don't you?"

"It's the gypsy in me," I said.

I told him everybody else was upstairs. Rafe said he'd wait until District Attorney Hackenbury got there before he called them down. He said he'd told the servant not to bother them.

"Our great D.A. would get sore as hell if we went ahead without him," he said. "We might get a little of the credit."

"In the absence of the bereaved relatives, permit me to appoint myself host. What's your pleasure?"

Bellows said he'd have rye, but Conner passed up the drink. I poured Bellows a drink, and he said, "Well, mud in your eye." He was a very original fellow.

Conner was watching me steadily. I tried to act as though I didn't notice. I did my best to sound casual as I asked, "With a murder on your hands, why the interest in simple arson?"

"That's what I'm here to find out," he said.

"So?"

"We identified the fellow on the train. Sent the fingerprints to New York, and they just called back he was Mickey Carr."

"That doesn't ring any bells with me."

"Just a punk. Six or seven arrests and a couple of convictions. Got out a year ago after a bit for extortion. Since then he's been bouncer at the Golden Mirror and chiseling what he could on the side."

That made me look up quickly. The next moment I could have kicked myself for falling for it.

"I had an idea that would click with you," Rafe said.

"I don't get you."

"I thought you'd remember the Golden Mirror. That's the night club where Miss Jones worked."

I still played dumb. "The girl on the train?"

"The young lady who was so interested in history she didn't recognize Carr."

"Hell, Rafe, just because she worked at the club doesn't mean …"

"Come off it, Tie. I don't know where you fit into this. Maybe you don't at all. But you do turn up in the damnedest places and the act you're putting on wouldn't fool a blind man."

"I don't know what you're driving at, Rafe, but if you're figuring me for a man of mystery …"

"All right, skip it," he said. "I'm here because we found out something else."

"Don't tell me you've discovered that I'm Jack the Ripper!"

"Are you?"

"I sometimes wonder." I gave my best imitation of a Murad advertisement, but it didn't go over so well. "What's the great discovery?"

"Maybe it doesn't mean a thing," he said, "but Dirck Wannerman was a passenger on that train."

"So were a few hundred other people."

"But the others didn't get burned to death in an arson fire the same day. That's why I came right out when the report this was a touch-off came in."

"How'd you find out that Wannerman was a passenger?"

"One of the others, fellow named Herkimer, saw him getting on the train. He remembered it because Wannerman snubbed him when he said hello and he tried to make something mysterious out of Wannerman's manner when we questioned him."

"Hell hath no fury like a Rotarian scorned."

Bellows looked puzzled. "That guy didn't say he was a Rotarian," he said.

The doorbell rang again. This time it was Assistant District Attorney Blosser and a couple of yes-men. Blosser had already got the lay from Chief Rainey. He and his stooges took over with a flourish, assembling everybody except Mrs. Wannerman and Paula in the living room. Ruth said she'd given Mrs. Wannerman a sedative and that the widow and her daughter were lying down. Blosser said he didn't guess it would be necessary to bother them until he'd talked to the rest of us.

"This is just preliminary, anyhow," he said. "Mr. Hackenbury will go into the matter fully after I make my report."

Blosser was your perfect yes-man. He never forgot Hackenbury was the boss and entitled to all the publicity, which was the only reason I could ever find for Blosser to have his job. Self-effacement is the first thing the Hackenburys of the world require of an assistant.

It didn't take me long to spiel my little piece about finding the tacks and the movie film. Then he turned to Ruth Overhart. Since nobody shooed me out, I slipped into a chair in a corner and did myself a spot of listening.

Ruth didn't have much to tell. She was a friend of the family and, of course, knew that Wannerman was trying to develop a process for making silk, but she didn't know much else about him.

"Mr. Wannerman wasn't a talkative person," she said. "He never said much about his affairs either in our personal or professional dealings."

"Professional?"

"He had trouble with his teeth and came to me. I suppose because I was the nearest dentist. I have my office in my home next door."

"Oh, yes, I see. Then you didn't know the family before they moved here."

She shook her head. "I met Mrs. Wannerman when

she came to me to have a tooth filled soon after they moved in. We liked each other, and we were neighbors, and ... well, we just became friends, I guess."

"As the family's closest friend, Dr. Overhart ..."

"I wouldn't call myself that, Mr. Blosser. We were friendly, but we weren't ... well, intimate. It's a little difficult to explain, I know, but I really didn't see very much of Mr. Wannerman or their daughter. He was usually busy with his work and Miss Wannerman spends a great deal of time in New York. I think she wanted to go on the stage or something like that, but her parents didn't approve, and I think she resented me because I agreed with them. So we never did get very close to each other, I'm afraid. I never thought of it before, but now that I do, I don't think I could tell you anything about Mr. Wannerman or his daughter. Mrs. Wannerman and I talked a great deal, but the rest of the family ..."

She broke off with an embarrassed little laugh. "I'm afraid that all sounds rather mixed up," she said.

"Not at all, Doctor, not at all." Blosser was nodding with what he obviously thought was an understanding manner. "I know exactly how such things are."

It struck me Ruth had taken a lot of words to say what I'd have expected her to put in a single sentence. She wasn't the kind who talked around a point as she'd done. And why had she dragged in Paula? Why had she made such a point of getting over that Paula resented her? Was it an attempt to discredit in advance something Paula might tell about her?

Blosser was thanking her, and Ruth was saying she was afraid she hadn't been much help, when Rafe Conner got up and bent over Blosser's shoulder. He whispered something, and Blosser looked flustered.

"Of course," he said. "Of course. I was just going to

ask Dr. Overhart."

Rafe went back to his chair, and Blosser turned to Ruth. She had stopped near the door and was facing him. She seemed strangely tense.

Blosser was saying, "I believe you said you were Mr. Wannerman's dentist? You have his dental chart, of course?"

"Why, yes. Naturally."

"Of course, naturally. You understand it will be necessary to identify the body by the dental work? I would appreciate it if ..."

"Certainly," she said. "I'll go over and get the chart now."

"Jarvis will go with you and bring it back. I don't want to trouble you more than necessary."

"It's no trouble at all. I was going home to lock up my house and then come back, anyway, to stay with Mrs. Wannerman tonight."

The watchman Nalor was next. He didn't add anything to what I already knew about Wannerman giving him the night off and his discovery of the fire when he came back to get the raincoat he'd forgotten.

"It's lucky I did, too, or the fire would've had such a start there wouldn't be nothing left," he said.

The maid, who doubled in brass as cook, had even less to tell. She said she'd been in the kitchen when she heard Nalor yelling that the lab was afire. She said she'd left the kitchen only once before that all evening.

"That was when these gentlemen came to see Mr. Wannerman," she said, nodding toward Sally Fiore and the big lug. "Mr. Wannerman was out in the laboratory and I was going to call him, but Mrs. Wannerman told me to go on with getting dinner ready, so I went back to the kitchen, and she called

Mr. Wannerman from the back door, but he didn't come in."

The others went out as they finished their stories, but I stayed put as Blosser turned to Fiore. The two shysters put on the usual Gaston-and-Alphonse act of a couple of chiseling lawyers on their professional behavior, but finally Sally Fiore got his story out. It was that he had advanced money to Wannerman to finance his experiments and that he'd motored out that evening from New York to see how the work was progressing. He said he was sitting with Mrs. Wannerman in the living room, waiting for Wannerman to come in from the lab, when they heard the watchman's shouts.

"A moment later there was an explosion," Fiore said, and he shook his head slowly. "It is a shocking tragedy."

Conner went over to Blosser and whispered to him again. Blosser frowned, but after a little more whispering from the detective, he nodded sagely as though he'd thought of it all along. He turned back to Fiore.

"I believe you were Mr. Wannerman's attorney?"

"Well," Fiore said, "yes and no. I represented Mr. Wannerman in a number of matters, but in the present instance I considered myself the representative of another client."

"I see," said Blosser, who obviously didn't. "As Mr. Wannerman's attorney, what would you say his financial status was?"

Fiore shrugged. "That's hard to say. He never discussed his affairs with me beyond the specific matter in which I represented him. I don't suppose it is unethical to say that matter concerned the incorporation of a company for the manufacture of his silk."

"Who were the other incorporators?"

Fiore smiled. "There weren't any. The matter never went that far. You see, Mr. Wannerman wanted to form a company to raise capital to perfect his process for commercial production of the silk, but it wasn't necessary."

"Wasn't necessary? I thought ..."

"A client of mine advanced the necessary capital. For, of course, a half interest in the process."

Conner broke in. "Let me get this straight. You never saw Wannerman until he came to you to incorporate a company to raise money to pay for his experiments? Then the company idea was discarded because one of your clients advanced him the money for a half interest in his process?"

"That's right."

"May I ask why you motored out this evening? I mean, was there any special reason for wanting to see Wannerman tonight?"

Again Fiore hesitated. Then he said, "Frankly, yes. My client was not satisfied with Mr. Wannerman's progress nor with his explanations for the delay in perfecting the process. So I telephoned Mr. Wannerman I would drive out this evening to get the matter settled."

"Settled?"

"To reach an understanding."

"And the fire beat you to it?"

"If you want to put it that way, yes."

"What was your idea of Wannerman's financial status?"

"I wouldn't like to guess. It was obvious, though, that his finances were limited or he wouldn't have had to raise outside capital to carry on his work."

"Did Wannerman carry fire insurance on his lab?"

"I don't think so. I think I would have known of it if he'd had any."

"How much did you say your client invested with Wannerman?"

"I didn't say. And I really don't see …"

"Just approximately? Five thousand? Ten?"

Fiore squirmed, hemming, and hawing, but finally, grudgingly, he said, "I suppose it would he in the neighborhood of twenty thousand. Maybe a little more."

"That's a lot of money to sink in a wildcat scheme, isn't it?"

"This wasn't a gamble. Before my client invested a dime, we saw the process in operation. We knew Wannerman could produce silk. We examined it fresh from his vat. There wasn't any doubt it was fine quality silk."

"Still," Conner said, "I'd think you'd have had Wannerman's life insured to protect the investment in just such a contingency as this, I mean, his death before perfecting his process."

Fiore looked unhappy, but he said, "Mr. Wannerman did insure his life. My client insisted on that, naturally."

"How much insurance did he carry?"

"I don't know whether he carried any besides this policy. It was for thirty thousand."

"And your client is the beneficiary?"

"Technically, I am. Of course, I am merely acting as my client's agent."

"Then it looks like your client stands to make a neat profit out of the deal even though the process wasn't perfected."

Fiore flushed. "I don't like your insinuation."

"I'm not insinuating anything," Rafe said, bland as

custard. "But your client will make ten thousand dollars profit if he collects the insurance."

Fiore's eyes narrowed. "Why shouldn't we collect?"

"What about the suicide clause? A smart insurance lawyer could make a pretty strong case arguing Wannerman tried to make a suicide appear to be an accidental death."

Fiore looked like a guy with aces back-to-back. "You're off on the wrong track," he said. "This policy's more than two years old, and the suicide clause runs only two years."

"Then this arrangement between Wannerman and your client is of long standing? I didn't understand that."

"You didn't ask," Fiore said. He was enjoying himself now. "If you had, I'd have told you."

Rafe ignored the chiseler's manner. He asked next whether Fiore's client had advanced the twenty thousand in a lump.

"As I recall it," Fiore said, "the first advance was five thousand. Mr. Wannerman thought that would be enough to defray his expenses, but technical difficulties developed, and he required more money, which my client advanced from time to time."

"You must have had a lot of faith in that process."

"We still have." Sally Fiore was the breed of pup who can't resist a chance to strut. "I think we won't have much difficulty finding a big silk company willing to pay handsomely for the process, even though it hasn't been developed to the point of commercial production yet."

"I guess you're right. It looks like your client gets all the good this ill wind blows. You've got your half in the process and you collect thirty thousand on the insurance and ..."

A woman's voice broke in: "I'm afraid there's a misunderstanding here."

It was Ruth Overhart. She was standing in the doorway with some big cards in her hands. They were the dental charts, and she gave them to Blosser, who was floundering in even deeper befuddlement than usual.

"I couldn't help overhearing," Ruth said, "and I thought I ought to straighten out the misunderstanding. Perhaps I shouldn't have spoken, but …"

"We are anxious to hear anything that will shed light on this tragedy," Blosser said. He still had the bewildered look of a lost and not especially bright child, but he was feeling better at being the center of things again. He beamed on Ruth as she sat down.

"I didn't think of it when I was here before, but I realize now I should have told you then," Ruth said. "You see, I'm the beneficiary of Mr. Wannerman's insurance."

Fiore jumped up. "You can't get away with that! I don't know what your game is, but …"

Conner stepped over and pushed him into his chair. Fiore was so excited he didn't know he'd been pushed. His big pal was looking dazed and dangerous.

"I'm sorry," Ruth said, "but I am. Mr. Wannerman changed the beneficiary of his policy six months ago."

Fiore burst out, "By God, you needn't think …"

"Shut up!" That was Rafe. He was standing in front of Ruth, frowning in a puzzled way. He didn't even glance at Fiore. The shyster glared at him, but subsided.

Rafe said, "Let's get this straight, Doctor. You say Wannerman changed his policy and made you the beneficiary six months ago. Why?"

"I invested twenty thousand dollars in his silk process. He said the insurance would protect me in the event of his death before perfecting it for commercial production."

"Then you stand to collect your investment and ten thousand profit."

"I mentioned that at the time, but Mr. Wannerman said … well …"

"Go ahead, Doctor. Just what did he say?"

"I don't know whether it's fair to repeat …"

"I'm afraid fairness doesn't enter into this, Doctor. We've got to get to the bottom of this mess, and the only way we can is to get all the facts before us."

"Well," Ruth said, "I don't pretend to know what Mr. Wannerman meant. But when he changed the policy, he said he was making me the sole beneficiary because he didn't want somebody else to profit by his death."

"Did he say who?" Rafe's voice was edged. Ruth hesitated and then shook her head.

"I'm sure he didn't mention a name. As I remember it, he said, 'I don't want them to get a penny from my death. They can kill me, but they won't collect for it.'"

"Doctor, you said you were not a close friend of Wannerman. Yet he confides in you that there's a chance he may be killed and makes you the beneficiary of thirty thousand dollars insurance. How do you make those jibe?"

Ruth flushed. "I'm sorry if you think I'm lying, but those are the facts. I invested my money because I saw the silk produced by his process and because I thought it was a good investment. I can't say why Mr. Wannerman made me the sole beneficiary, but I'd have been a fool to refuse."

"I agree with you. Thirty thousand for twenty is a good profit."

"It is." Her eyes didn't waver as she looked at Rafe. There were two fiery red spots on her cheeks. Her voice was icy as she said, "Is there anything else you wish to ask me?"

"Just one thing, Doctor. Did Wannerman mention why he didn't get the additional money he needed from his original backer?"

"He said he was afraid to ask for more."

"Afraid?"

"He told me that somebody had forced him to accept their financial backing. This person had threatened him because he had not yet perfected his process."

"What did he mean by forced?"

"He told me he was given his choice of selling half interest in his process or ..."

"Or?"

She took a deep breath. "I know it sounds melodramatic, but it's the truth. Mr. Wannerman told me he had to sell half interest in his process or be killed."

Fiore fairly screamed, "This is outrageous! I won't stand for these insulting lies about ..."

"Keep quiet!" Rafe's voice stopped Fiore like a fist. For a moment the detective stood silent and then he said, "You realize, Dr. Overhart, the implications of what you've said?"

She shook her head. "I am merely repeating what Mr. Wannerman told me. You can believe me or not, as you choose."

"Did Mr. Wannerman carry fire insurance?"

"No, he didn't. Mrs. Wannerman told me she tried to persuade him to, but he refused."

"Don't you think it was strange that Mr. Wannerman should make you the beneficiary of his insurance and leave his family unprovided for?"

Ruth stood up. Her voice was level, cold.

"That is not my affair," she said. "And I do not intend to listen to any more of your crude insults."

Blosser broke in, blurting befuddled apologies, assuring Dr. Overhart that Mr. Conner hadn't meant to be insulting to anybody. Rafe just looked at Ruth and didn't say anything. He stuck a fresh piece of gum in his mouth.

"Since you are so interested in the matter," Ruth said, "I would suggest that you ask Mrs. Wannerman. I believe she has a small but adequate income from a trust fund set up by her father."

"Thank you, Doctor, we …"

"Now, if you are through with me, I will go upstairs to Mrs. Wannerman."

Blosser looked at Rafe, but the detective kept a poker face as Ruth walked out of the room and started up the stairs. Then he turned to Fiore.

"Well," he said, "it looks like your client's not going to get such a haul, after all."

"She can't get away with it. We won't stand …"

"I've got an idea you'll have to," Rafe said. "Now, let's get on with this."

Blosser looked resentful at the way Rafe Conner had taken charge of the questioning, but he obviously didn't know what to do about it, so he just sat there and looked vacant. Rafe nodded toward the big lug on the couch and said, "This gentleman came with you, Mr. Fiore?"

"Yes, of course. He's … he's my chauffeur."

"I see." He turned to the lug. "Were you outside in the car when the fire started."

"Naw, I was in here with Sally."

"Sally?"

"Him, Fiore."

Conner turned back to the lawyer. "Wasn't it rather unusual to bring your chauffeur in with you?"

Fiore flushed. "I don't see what bearing ..."

"Don't get excited. I'm just asking."

"I ... I told him to come inside because ... well ..."

"Yes?"

"I ... well, I didn't know how Mr. Wannerman would take it when I demanded a complete report, and I thought ..."

"You thought you'd have your chauffeur handy in case of trouble?"

"That's it exactly. You see, there was nothing unusual about it. Nothing strange, I mean."

"Do your servants usually call you Sally?"

"I ... really ..."

"Skip it," Rafe said. He didn't seem to notice that Fiore, for all his air of injured dignity, was visibly relieved at escaping more questions about the big guy. The lug started to grin, but caught himself and went deadpan. His name was Elmer Hodges. At least, that was one of his names. It turned out that he had a lot of others.

Rafe whispered to Blosser again, and Blosser said, "I guess that's all we can do now. You gentlemen have been very helpful. Thank you. I'm sure you won't mind coming out if Mr. Hackenbury wishes to talk to you."

"Not at all," Fiore said. "Glad to help. Just call on me."

"Sure," said the big lug.

They got up, and Fiore and Blosser went through a handshaking act, and then Fiore started for the door in Elmer's wake.

"Just a second," Rafe said, and Fiore turned. "This client of yours who financed Wannerman. Was he, by any chance, Nicky Pet?"

Sally Fiore went beet-red. Elmer's jaw sagged. Fiore tried to bluster, but Rafe cut him short.

"I am not at liberty to reveal the identity of my client. I assure you his identity has no bearing …"

"Let me be the judge of that. It was Nicky Pet who put up the money?"

Fiore was floundering, and Elmer was glaring at me. I had the unpleasant realization that Elmer figured I had tipped Conner that Fiore was Nicky Pet's lawyer. That could be damned embarrassing. I tried to look innocent, but it didn't go over with Elmer. Nor with Fiore, either, when he glanced at me.

Rafe cut off Fiore's jabber by saying, "Either Nicky put up the dough or he didn't? Which was it?"

Fiore changed signals. He shrugged as though the matter wasn't of the slightest importance.

"On my advice as his attorney, Mr. Petrocoli did advance the money. But he had no interest in …"

"Twenty grand's not chicken feed."

Fiore was playing upstage now. "To a man of Mr. Petrocoli's wide interests, twenty thousand dollars is hardly a major item," he said.

"Maybe you're right, but I always heard Nicky Pet hated to lose a dollar as much as an arm."

"I assure you …"

"Okay, I guess I got a bum steer. Good night."

Fiore and Elmer went out, and Blosser's stooges, neither of whom had chirped through the questioning, began bustling about now, putting their notebooks in their pockets and pushing chairs back into place. Blosser said he guessed they'd done all they could.

"What about Wannerman's papers?" Rafe said. "Hadn't we better have a look at them?"

"I don't see any need for rush about this. It's a simple case of arson that backfired on the arsonist."

"What motive did he have for arson?" Rafe objected. "His lawyer and his wife say he didn't carry any fire insurance."

"He might not have told them about it," Blosser said.

"Of course, we'll have to check on that. But our information now from two sources is that there wasn't any fire insurance. If that's right, why should Wannerman set fire to his laboratory?"

Blosser floundered and hemmed and ended up by asking, "Why do you think he did it?"

"Maybe he didn't," Rafe said.

Blosser and his stooges gawked at the detective.

"If our information about the fire insurance is right, and I see no reason to doubt it yet, Wannerman had no apparent motive for arson. But others did."

"You mean ..."

"I mean Nicky Pet and Dr. Overhart each had thirty thousand reasons to commit murder and try to cover it up by burning the body so we would think Wannerman had been killed by an explosion of his chemicals."

"Oh, come now, you're being farfetched about this."

"Maybe, but if it was murder, it was mighty near perfect."

Blosser looked more and more miserable under the strain of actually trying to think. Conner turned to me and asked if I'd mind leaving them alone.

"I wondered why you didn't shoo me before," I said, getting up.

"Thought you might be interested in hearing what everybody had to say," he replied. "Weren't you?"

"So-so. It was mostly over my head."

"That's too bad," Rafe said quietly. His tone could have meant any of a dozen things, but there was no hint in his expression what it did mean. Rafe Conner made the Great Stone Face seem like an open book.

I went out in the hall and reached in my pocket for a cigarette. I touched the red calot. I wondered what Rafe would have said if I'd told him of my encounter in the thicket. I'd have given every sou I possessed at that moment to have known whether Rafe Conner remembered that Pa had a set of Gurkha knives with elephant heads carved on the hilts. As I paced slowly up and down the hall, waiting for Rafe to break up the conference, I had the uncomfortable feeling that I'd got myself out on the end of a limb and Rafe Conner was sharpening a saw.

I don't remember who mentioned that Wannerman used an extra bedroom upstairs as an office, but somebody had. I got to wondering what they would find in his papers. I had the jitters so bad that it seemed logical to me that maybe when Rafe and the D.A.'s dopes started going through his papers they'd find the answers. Maybe they'd even find the reason why a knife from our house was used to cut Fish Eye's throat. For there must be some connection between the screwy Wannerman setup and the murder on the train. If there wasn't, what was Fish Eye's pal Gretchen Jones doing snooping around the Wannerman yard in the dark? And what significance was there to Wannerman's presence on the train?

I did a fool thing then, but I was nearly nuts worrying about that Gurkha knife. I couldn't take a chance that Wannerman's papers contained a tip-off that would point to our house. So I went quietly up the stairs to have a look through Wannerman's papers before Rafe and Blosser

I was jumpy enough to yell, thinking of the chance that they'd come up in a few minutes. But I figured I had to risk it.

There were seven doors opening onto the upstairs hall, and I didn't have the wooziest notion which was the door to Wannerman's office. I stopped at the first door to listen. I heard voices. That would be Mrs. Wannerman's room, and I guessed Ruth was talking to her.

I held my breath at the next door, pressing my ear against the panel, but I couldn't hear a sound. That didn't mean Paula Wannerman wasn't inside, though. Or the maid, if she slept upstairs.

I couldn't stand there all night. I had to go through with it or scram. And if somebody was inside, I could say I'd come upstairs hunting for Ruth. They might wonder why I didn't knock before stalking into rooms, but they'd just have to wonder. I couldn't risk a knock.

I opened the door and stepped inside. The room was dark, but by the light in the hall behind me I saw it wasn't a bedroom. I was getting a break. I'd hit it right the first try. I closed the door soundlessly behind me and felt along the wall until I found the switch. It turned on a green-shaded student's lamp on a big desk shoved up under a wide window looking out over the side yard. I saw there was a key in the lock and for a moment I was tempted to lock the door, but I didn't. My gag about hunting for Ruth was weak enough without having to explain a locked door.

There was a second door in the room. I stood a moment staring at it as though it were going to bite me. My luck still held, though. It was on the opposite side from the room in which I'd heard the voices. I tiptoed over to the door and knelt down. I squinted through the keyhole. It was my third pass: the room beyond was dark.

I stood up and looked around Wannerman's office. It was a drab, brownish room. There wasn't much furniture: a couple of glassed, sectional bookcases crammed with books and magazines; a couple of straight chairs and a dilapidated easy chair; a big flat-topped desk pushed up against the two windows at the far end of the room; a greenish steel filing cabinet with three drawers.

I turned to the filing cabinet first. I had to work fast. At any moment, Blosser and Rafe might finish their confab and come upstairs. At any moment, somebody else might get the notion of coming to the office.

The top drawer of the cabinet didn't make a sound. It was empty. I tried the other drawers. They contained only a few cardboard folders. They'd obviously been used, but somebody had stripped them of whatever they'd contained.

I turned to the desk. The top drawer stuck. I tried to yank it, and it squeaked loudly. I froze. I held my breath, straining my ears for the sound of someone coming. I relaxed slowly. It must have sounded so loud to me because I had the jitters. I let the drawer stay stuck, though, and pulled out the second. It contained only a batch of stationery, a few pencils, a bottle of ink and some pens, a box of paper clips, and some hundreds of rubber bands. The other drawers were empty. If there'd been any papers in that desk, somebody had sure done a good job of emptying it.

I went over to the bookcases. Most of the books and magazines seemed to be technical: about silk, textiles generally, chemistry. I was trying to decide whether to risk the time I'd need to examine the books when I saw something that made me forget all about them. It was the wastebasket: a squarish, metal basket beside the easy chair. And the bottom of the basket was thick with burned paper.

I stepped over and bent down, poking with my fingers in the charred rubbish. I felt a sharp disappointment. It was all burned except for a few ends and corners, and they didn't seem to be any help. The only scrap which wasn't blank was about half the size of a postal card and seemed to be what was left of a bill. I picked it up, dusting off the ash. There were only a few words on it:

Below the printed heading I could see a couple of lines of handwriting, but the paper was so browned and curling that I couldn't make out the words. I started to drop the scrap back into the wastebasket, but checked myself. There was something familiar about … LEWITE & COH … but I couldn't make it click in my head.

And the word beginning *Si?* Of course, I was dumb not to have spotted that right off. What could the word be except *silk?* Then I remembered with a jolt. That big book Gretchen Jones had been reading on the train. I'd spotted the letters SI. Why was she reading a book on silk?

I was sure that somehow, somewhere in the back of my head, *Hepplewite* was mixed up with Gretchen Jones, but I couldn't drag it out. I slipped the paper into my wallet. I tried the stuck drawer again. In a burst of irritation, I yanked it sharply. It came open so suddenly, I almost fell over backwards. The noise it made cooled me off pronto. Everybody in the house must be deaf not to have heard it. That's how loud it sounded to me. I waited, but there was no sound of anybody coming. I began rummaging in the drawer.

There wasn't much in it: just some old bills, all neatly bundled with rubber bands. There were light bills, grocery bills, clothing bills. I went over the bills. Wannerman had paid $90 the month before for an overcoat and he'd bought a dozen pair of socks. He'd paid $33 and some cents to a liquor store, $3.70 to a hardware store, $2.40 to the gas company, $5.80 to a drugstore, $4.67 to the electric company. All of which might have been interesting to his biographer, but it didn't help me. I dropped the bills back in the drawer and ...

A voice behind me said, "If you move, I'll kill you!"

Chapter Six

The voice behind me spoke again. It was a cold voice. A woman's voice. It said, "Put up your hands and turn around. Don't think you can rush me because I'll shoot you before you can take a step."

I obeyed, turning slowly. The woman was Paula Wannerman. She had come through the side door from the dark room beyond. She was standing in the doorway now. Her hair was tumbled and she wore a black negligee that didn't hide much, if anything. I was, however, too preoccupied with the ugly little revolver she was pointing at me to have much interest in any anatomy except my own. When she spoke again, I noticed her voice was fuzzy around the edges. She swayed a little. She was tight as a tick. I wondered if she was tight enough for me to try rushing her. She was only five steps away. Maybe I could get to her before she could fire. I didn't try, though. There was something discouraging about the way she held the gun.

I finally dragged my voice up from the soles of my shoes and said, "I was looking for Dr. Overhart. I thought …"

"Dear Ruth does get in the quaintest places, doesn't she?"

"I …"

"But I hardly think even Ruth would be hiding in a drawer, do you?"

Her eyes were narrowed. Her mouth was twisted into a cold little smile.

"I suppose I'll have to shoot you," she said.

My legs were shaking. My throat was dry. I couldn't say anything as she stood there, toying with the idea of pulling the trigger. If she did, the bullet would hit me in the gut. I had to say something. I had to talk her out of it. I saw a guy once with a belly wound. It took him a long time to die.

I tried to make my voice sound casual. Maybe she was drunk enough to be kidded out of it.

"The cops don't approve of murder," I said. "And this house is lousy with cops."

"It isn't murder to shoot a burglar."

"I'm hardly …"

"What are you, then? A Baptist missionary? Maybe you were hunting for converts in my father's desk?"

"You've got the wrong idea," I said. It was time to talk fast. The muzzle of the gun was steadier. She was just drunk enough to blast me for the fun of it.

"If you'll just point that gun somewhere else, I can explain the whole thing," I said. "It makes me nervous. I know this looks bad, but if you'll …"

"Sorry, but I'm not taking any chances." The icy smile faded and her mouth grew taut.

"I warned you, Boy Scout. Now you've got to take your medicine."

A door slammed out in the hall. The sound startled her. She glanced quickly at the door of the room. I flung myself forward. It was an automatic reaction. All I remembered afterward was the hate blazing in her green eyes when her head swung back and she saw me. I hit her wrist and the gun dropped.

She clawed at me, but I grabbed her arm and jerked her forward. She spun around. I grabbed her from behind, one arm around the waist and the other, around her neck. I clapped my hand over her mouth to keep her from screaming. She bit. I jerked my hand away. She was struggling furiously, trying to kick my shins, trying to wrench herself out of my grasp. She was panting.

"God damn you ... damn you!"

She didn't scream, though. Even in those bedlam moments I wondered why she didn't. Then suddenly she went limp in my arms. I thought for a moment she had passed out, but she hadn't. She'd just given up trying to get away. She sagged against my arm and she couldn't speak for a little while for lack of breath. Then she said, "It's your move, Boy Scout."

I didn't say anything. I was too busy trying to decide what to do. I couldn't stand there holding her all night, and I couldn't let her go. I guessed the door we'd heard slam meant Rafe Conners and Blosser were coming upstairs, but I couldn't hear anything. That was a break. If the walls were that thick, maybe nobody had heard me tussling with Paula Wannerman. I had to move fast, though. They'd be coming in at any second. I had to gamble the drunk girl didn't squawk. I kept my voice at a whisper.

"If you keep your mouth shut, you won't get hurt and I'll give you the whole lay," I said. "I don't know what your angle is, but we can work together. Get in that next room, and if you make a sound, I'll break your neck."

It was all just words, and I didn't have much hope it'd keep her quiet, but there wasn't anything else I could do. I started her toward the side door through which she had come and I switched off the light. I picked up the pistol as I followed, closing the door gently behind me.

She was strangely silent. I could see her only dimly by the street light that filtered through a big tree rising up across her windows. I closed my left hand on her wrist, and she didn't struggle. I hesitated, trying to decide what my next move should be.

I put my arm around her. Maybe she thought it was affection, but I wanted to have a good grip on her if she tried anything. I didn't want to have to chase her around that dark room. A moment later, we heard voices in Wannerman's office. I couldn't make out the words, though.

I was barely conscious of the girl as we stood there in the darkness beside the door, trying to hear what was being said. We caught a word now and then, but not enough to make any sense. I guessed from the rumble of the voices, though, that Ruth was inside with Rafe and Blosser. They were there a long time and then we didn't hear them anymore.

The girl whispered, "They've gone."

I realized then that my arm had been tight around her waist. I relaxed it, and I heard her take a deep breath in the dark. Her voice was a sort of muffled gasp.

"You're the strongest Boy Scout I ever ..."

"Ssshhh!"

I had to take a chance she wouldn't conk me over the head. I bent down and looked through the keyhole. The office beyond was dark. I straightened up. My nerves began to unwind.

"We can relax," I said. "Sorry I held you so tight."

From the dark came a warm, throaty chuckle. "I'm not," she said. I heard her move across the room. She wasn't whispering now. "Shall we have some light on the subject?"

I hesitated. She said, "It's all right. They'll think I'm drinking myself to sleep as usual."

I felt a sharp suspicion. The change in her was too sudden. But I had to play 'em as they lay. I said, "Okay, go ahead."

She fumbled a moment, and then one of the shaded lights on her dressing table went on. We were in her bedroom, a cluttered, frilly room, and on the bedside table was a bottle of Scotch, a siphon and a dish of ice.

She was standing beside the dressing table, looking at me with lazy green eyes. Our struggle had tousled her hair even more and torn her negligee off one shoulder. She didn't make any attempt to cover it. She smiled slowly and sat down at the dressing table.

"Fix a couple of drinks and we'll toast our armistice," she said. "I'll try to remove the marks of battle."

She was watching me in the mirror as she did things to her hair, and I felt like a sap. I was still holding the pistol and she said, "Don't you think you can put up the artillery?"

I slipped the pistol in my coat pocket and turned to the table to mix a couple of drinks. I heard her move behind me and whirled around. She was locking the door to the hall. She laughed softly.

"I wouldn't hurt you," she said, and she came slowly toward me. "Not for worlds."

I stopped her by sticking a highball out to her. She was surprised, and then a little amused, and she said, "Don't tell me you're Sir Galahad."

I skipped it. "Here's how," I said, lifting my glass.

She sat down on the fluffy bed. We were drinking when we were frozen by somebody knocking on the door. I took a step forward on an impulse to keep her from calling out, but she was too quick for me. She asked who it was.

"It's Ruth. Something's happened."

I could see the knob turn as Ruth tried to come in, and I blessed the luck that had made the blonde lock the door.

"All right," Paula called. "I'll be out."

She got up and motioned me to a closet. She moved around as though getting out of bed to cover the sound of my tiptoeing to the closet. She put her hand on my shoulder as I stepped inside.

"Get out while I'm gone," she whispered. "I'll try to keep the coast clear."

Her hand slid suddenly up the back of my neck and pulled my head down to her mouth. She kissed me. I stood like a bloody fool with the highball in my hand.

Ruth called, "Hurry, Paula. Open the door."

Paula whispered, "That's to bind the bargain. I'll phone you later." To Ruth she called, "All right, all right, I'm getting up!"

She squeezed my arm and closed the closet door, leaving me standing in the dark in a mess of dresses and coats and the faint odor of perfume. I held my breath, straining to hear as Paula opened the door to her room. I heard her say, "What's the trouble?" I heard Ruth say, "The detective has to talk to you."

The closing of the door to the room as the women went out into the hall cut off the rest of what she was saying. I stood a few moments longer in the closet. Then I opened the door slowly. I went over to the door and listened, but I couldn't hear a thing. I opened it a crack and peered out into the hallway. There wasn't a sign of anybody around. I stepped outside, praying to God I didn't step on a creaky plank, and hurried downstairs. The door to the living room was shut and I was tempted to stop and try to listen, but by this time I was too jittery. I had to get out of that house or go nuts. I didn't begin breathing naturally again until I was home and closed the front door behind me and started up the stairs.

I went back to the library. Pa was still there, sprawled out in his chair with a drink in his hand. He glanced up as I came in and said, "You've been quite a time, son."

"Things have been happening," I said, flopping in a chair.

"Messalina went over for a little while to see if she could help. She tells me Wannerman was burned."

"To a cinder. But that's not the half of it. It was arson. Went up quicker than he expected, I guess, and caught him. That girl on the train's mixed up in it somehow. I tell you, Pa, it's running me bughouse."

Pa got up and brought another siphon of seltzer from the case in the corner. He walked straight, though I knew he had enough liquor aboard to float the *Normandie*. He settled down in his chair again, stretching out his lanky legs, and he smoothed his droopy grey moustache with skinny fingers, an absent-minded gesture of his when he was doing some heavy thinking. He sipped his drink and sank even lower in the chair.

"Suppose you tell me what happened, son. I've got an idea we've got to work fast. From what I remember of him, your friend Conner is nobody's fool."

"If you know where to start, you know more than I do," I said. "Conner's already got ideas—about us. About me, anyhow."

"He'll need more than ideas, son."

"You may be right, Father Sherlock, but your filial Watson is a lot less optimistic. Do you realize Messalina or …"

"Or me or any one of us," he broke in. "Certainly I realize that any one of us might have given the knife to the murderer and that you might be the murderer. That's why we've got to clear this up before Conner tumbles to the possibility, too. I think I mentioned that earlier."

So I told my crazy story, leaving out nothing, not even the smallest detail of what I've put down here. Pa didn't move while I talked, didn't give any sign that he even heard me. Even when I finished, he didn't say anything for a long time. Finally, he chuckled. My nerves were so jangled that I flared up at him.

"What's so funny?" I snapped. "Let me in on the joke."

"I have just seen the first gleam of light through the mystery," he said.

"What is it? It's a cinch I don't see any light or anything funny, either, about this mess."

"I must disagree with you, son. It has distinct elements of ironic humor."

He wouldn't tell me what he'd doped out, though I deviled him to let me in on it. He seemed to be enjoying himself, which didn't improve my humor.

"Suppose," he said at last, "That Wannerman was the murderer on the train. Doesn't that open a lot of interesting theories to you?"

"I'm not interested in theories, but that one's cockeyed. How could he have got our knife?"

"Ruth Overhart could have given it to him. She is often in our house and she is his friend."

"So are some of Messalina's D.A.R. dames, I guess. But it's just as crazy to suspect Ruth as it is to suspect them."

"Is it any crazier than suspecting Messalina or Cal or either of us?"

"No, but ... damn it, Pa, Ruth just doesn't fit in as a murderer's accomplice."

"Murderer's accomplices seldom do," he said. "It is a prime requisite for a successful accomplice."

"But what reason on God's green earth could Wannerman have for murdering Fish Eye?"

"You disappoint me, son. Of course, we can't know yet with certainty. But if the facts you have gathered don't give you a firm basis for a mighty good guess ..."

"Cut out the riddles, Pa, can't you? I don't feel like playing a guessing game. What're you driving at."

"I suggest you ask your friend Gretchen Jones. She could tell you, I'm pretty sure."

"Which doesn't mean she would tell me."

"I rather think she will, if you're ... tactful."

I didn't like the way he paused before that last word. I looked at him sharply and asked, "Just what do you mean, tactful?"

"That depends on Miss Jones. We'll start with her when we go to town tomorrow."

"I didn't know we were going."

"Oh, yes, indeed. I am visiting you indefinitely. Until we've cleared this up. I think Conner will do everything we could out here. Our place to work is in New York. And the place to start is Miss Jones."

"Maybe you know what you're doing, but the deeper we get, the more hopeless it looks to me. The girl isn't the talking kind, either."

Pa smiled softly. "She may become more communicative when you return her red hat. I think she will prefer to explain to us instead of to the police."

Messalina tapped on the door and came in. She said somebody wanted me on the telephone. As I started for the kitchen, I asked her, "How's Cal?"

"He's still asleep. He ought to know by this time that he just can't drink."

It was Paula Wannerman calling. She said the detective had wanted to find out why her father went to town, and she couldn't tell them.

"They're trying to mix him up in that murder on the train," she said. "Somebody saw him getting on the train in New York, but it seems he wasn't on it when it got to Scraffton. At least, he didn't give his right name, if he was."

"Don't worry about it. The man may have made a mistake or your father may have got off at another station."

"Oh, I'm not worried about my dear parent. I just don't want anything to happen that'll make my mother more miserable. He was a damned beast, but she loved him."

She paused a moment and then she said, "I've got to see you, Boy Scout. There's some things we've got to get settled."

"I'm going back to the city the first thing in the morning."

"I'll come to town tomorrow night then. When can I meet you?"

It occurred to me that there were a lot of answers I wanted that Paula Wannerman probably could give me, and so I said, "I'll meet you wherever you say."

"Do you know a place called the Golden Mirror?"

That jolted me. The Golden Mirror was the night club where Fish Eye was bouncer and where Gretchen Jones had worked. Why, of all the places in New York, did Paula Wannerman pick that one for our meeting?

"I'll meet you there at eight," I said.

"I've never been there, but I've got a special reason for wanting to be there tomorrow night."

"That sounds pretty mysterious. What's the reason?"

She laughed. "I'll let you guess that," she said. "Maybe I'll tell you tomorrow—if you tell me the things I want to know."

She hung up, and I went back to sit with Pa. I didn't realize until then just how tired I was. In a little while, I turned in, leaving Pa sitting beside the window, smiling to himself at this secret he wouldn't tell me, a secret he said he'd drawn from the story I told him. When I was in bed, I went again and again over every detail of my story to Pa, but I still didn't tumble to the tell-tale fact that he'd snapped up at once.

Pa woke me up early the next morning. He had a newspaper in his hand. He was frowning in a sort of preoccupied way.

"We've got to make tracks, son. Conner's not letting any grass grow under his feet."

"What's he done now?"

"He's had the body identified, for one thing. It's definitely identified as Wannerman. They checked the dental charts at the morgue, and the dead man's teeth tally down to the last filling."

"We knew that already," I said.

"Here's something we didn't know. Wannerman died from an air thrombosis. The paper says they rushed the autopsy through last night."

"Air thrombosis? That doesn't mean a thing to me."

"Dirck Wannerman was murdered," he said. "Somebody shot a bubble of air into a vein—and it stopped his heart."

Chapter Seven

My brother Caligula managed to get downstairs to give me a wan handshake by way of greeting and farewell. He didn't seem glad to see me or disappointed that I was leaving. The intensity of his hangover made it impossible for him to look anything except miserable. Messalina said that for the first time in ten years Cal was staying home from his shop. He'd had her telephone his clerk that he had the grippe. Cal kept an optical shop in New York, incidentally, and later moved there.

Pa didn't mention the murders on the train and when we got to my two-rooms-and-bath on Jane Street, I urged drinks on him in the hope the liquor would take his mind off Gretchen Jones and I'd be able to get some shuteye. Pa was a perpetual Barkis when it came to whiskey, but he didn't let me turn in.

"Get over to the Jones girl's house right away," he said. "If you hang around, Conner or somebody else may beat you to her."

"What good will that do? Do you think she'll sit down and sign a confession for me? Maybe she'll even hire a public stenographer to save me the trouble of taking it down."

"Maybe," he said.

What I said wasn't printable. I knew I was licked, though. I never won an argument from Pa yet. He could argue the gold fillings out of a miser's teeth.

The only hope I had as I walked down toward Commerce Street was that the red calot in my pocket might panic her so she'd talk.

"I wouldn't tell her about the hat at first," Pa told me. "If she knows it was you in the thicket, she'll suspect you've got it, but she'll be hoping it was lost in the scuffle and you didn't find it. And a woman's wish is almost invariably father to her thought, so she'll probably spin you a yarn based on the supposition that you don't know she was the woman in the thicket. Then, when you spring the hat on her, it'll be a tougher thing for her to explain. She'll have to fit it into a story she's already told instead of having the comparatively simple task of telling her story so as to include an explanation of the hat."

He was pouring another drink for himself and he looked so serenely at peace with the world that I wanted to paste him one or something.

"I hope you get the D.T.'s," I said, and slammed the door as I went out.

The address Gretchen Jones had given Conner, and which she'd proved by showing letters and a credit card, was one of those old red brick houses, four or five stories high, with three one-room, kitchenette and bath apartments on each floor. I pushed her bell four or five times, but there wasn't any answer. I was as relieved as a man who looks under the bed and doesn't find a burglar. I didn't want to see her or anybody else. All I wanted to do was to go home and sleep.

I remembered that she'd said she used to sing at the Golden Mirror, so I got a taxi and went there. I knew that if I turned up at home so soon, Pa would get the idea of running me over to the Golden Mirror to check up on her.

All I knew about the Golden Mirror was that it was

a Village gyp joint greatly favored by politicians and visiting firemen. It had a floor show that would have sizzled their whiskers, if they'd had any, but there wouldn't be anything doing in the afternoon. Suckers were too busy then earning dough so they'd be worth plucking at night.

The bar was open, but that was all. The bar faced the street, and you had to go through it to reach the club proper beyond. The only people I saw in the joint were a bartender with a jaundiced eye and a skinny customer with the willies. The bartender was reading a racing paper down at the far end of the bar, paying no attention to the customer, who was uttering all over the place in his efforts to get a whiskey sour to his mouth without spilling it. The bartender gave me a Scotch and soda as though he resented the interruption and went back to his racing chart. It was a cinch I'd get nothing out of that Sour Puss. The guy with the jim-jams looked even less hopeful. So I just stood there and waited, nursing my drink. The other customer finally got his drink down and wove out of the place. Sour Puss didn't even look up from his paper.

There was no reason for me to waste any more time there, but I knew that as sure as I went home, Pa would think of something for me to do. It was more restful to perch on a stool at the bar and nurse along my drink. I couldn't stay there forever, though, and finally I went to the telephone booth at the far end of the bar and dialed my home number. I muffed it the first time because there wasn't any light. I blasted the phone company, but the next moment I was ready to burn candles in thankfulness that there wasn't any light. For through the glass panel of the door, I saw Gretchen Jones and a man come in. She didn't notice me because there wasn't a light in the booth.

I got just a flash of her face as she sat down with her back toward me at a table against the wall. It was the face of a woman at the breaking point. She was wearing another red calot. She must have had a passion for them. Well, she knew what suited her, anyhow.

The man sat down across the table from her. The glass panel of the booth door made a frame through which I watched his face. He was a dark, slick guy with about as much forehead as a rat. He wore a natty green suit with belt on the back of his coat and tucks at his waist. They'd been arguing when they came in, and he started in again the moment they sat down. He stopped when the bartender came over. The bartender seemed to know them. He brought the man a highball and the girl a Manhattan, and then he disappeared from my line of vision in the direction of the bar. I guessed he'd gone back to his racing charts.

Tuck Waist took an angry swig of his drink and leaned forward across the table, talking a mile a minute. Any casting director in the world would have leaped at him for a gangster role. I put him down for the sort of punk who shakes down two-bit limit stud games and tries to act like movie gangsters.

The girl didn't touch her drink. The guy snapped something at her and lifted his glass. The girl leaned a little forward, talking earnestly, making little gestures of emphasis with one hand. His face showed he had her pegged for a liar.

At that moment, Pa answered the phone: "Hello."

I said, "Call you later," and hung up. I kept my hand on the receiver. If anybody came by and took a look into the booth, I could be just making another call.

I pushed the phone booth door carefully open about

an inch and strained to hear what Tuck Waist and the Jones dame were saying, but I couldn't. They were keeping their voices too low. The girl couldn't see me, and I was dead sure Tuck Waist hadn't noticed that somebody was in the phone booth, so I guessed they didn't want their pal Sour Puss to hear what they were rowing about.

It was hell not to be able to get even a line on what they were saying, but I had to be content with what I could guess from Tuck Waist's face, which was that they were getting hotter every second. If I went out of the booth and near enough to hear, it was light years to a second that she would hustle him off.

The guy was getting sorer by the minute. Every time the girl tried to speak, he cut her off and started in again with the kind of ugly, wise guy expression it would have been a pleasure to wipe off his mug.

Then everything started happening at once. I was wishing I'd brought my drink with me to the phone booth when Tuck Waist leaned quickly toward the girl and snapped something. His eyes were murderous. The girl's voice rose sharply.

"I didn't! I've told you I didn't!"

He exploded. His hand swung so swiftly that I didn't really see it, but I heard the smack of his palm on the girl's face. I heard him yell, "You're a lying bitch!" I heard the girl cry out from the blow.

I tumbled out of the booth. God knows what made me do it. I got across that barroom before Tuck Waist knew I was there. I didn't give him a chance to get up. I swung on him with everything I had. I had a flash of his astounded face. At that instant my fist smashed against his nose. He banged back against the wall. His head hit with a loud crack. He yelled. He was trying to get up. Blood was spurting from his nose. I gave it to him again. I wanted to kill the bastard.

There was blood on the tablecloth. His head bumped there when he went back the second time. He was trying to get something out of his hip pocket.

I lunged over the table. I grabbed him by the shirtfront and yanked him up. He was sobbing, cursing. He hit me a couple of times. I didn't feel the blows. This time I wasn't going to miss the button.

I heard the girl scream as I swung. I couldn't stop. My fist smeared his face as she hurled her glass. It showered me with the cocktail as it shot past.

Tuck Waist crashed down under the table and I whirled to face the bartender. He'd been coming at me with the ice club when the girl's glass hit him in the face.

It was a lucky shot. It wasn't enough to stop him, but it threw him just long enough for me to whirl. The stick was swinging. I rushed under it. God knows how. I heard him grunt as I grabbed him.

I yelled to the girl to run. Sour Puss and I went down. The smack nearly jarred my teeth loose. But I was on top. So it must have jarred him more. He was still fighting, though. He was smaller than I, but a fighting fool. I knew I couldn't hold him. I knew he'd throw me off him in a second. The jolt had me foggy. I was licked and I knew it.

We rolled over, clawing at each other. I ended up on top again. My lungs were aching. I was gasping. I couldn't hold him another second. The strength was slipping from me. And he knew it. His eyes showed it. Slowly, slowly, he was pushing back my head. I thought my neck was breaking.

I grabbed below his belt.

I heard him scream.

He went limp, twisting on the floor.

I scrambled groggily, weakly, to my feet. He was holding himself with both hands as he lay there, gasping like a fish.

It was all whirling around. I snatched up my hat and stumbled toward the door. The guy under the table was coming to. He was crawling out. His face was smeared with blood. He had a gun. He was trying to pull it from his pocket.

I still don't know just what happened in those next moments. I was out on my feet. Somebody grabbed my arm. Somebody was dragging me along the street. It was Gretchen Jones. We tumbled into a cab. It made a lot of noise starting. I could hear somebody shouting behind us, but it seemed a long way off. The cab swung around a lot of corners and then it stopped. The jolt snapped my head back. The girl was saying, "Get out! Hurry!"

I stood on the curb and saw her pay the driver. He looked at us funny. She took my arm and then we were walking through the crowd. I saw the elevated trestle and I heard a train rattle-banging above us, so I knew we were on Third Avenue. My head was hurting. I felt sick at the stomach.

We stopped at the corner and she opened the door of a waiting cab. She said, "Get in," and we got in the cab. She said something to the driver, and then we were moving. I wondered where we were going, but it didn't seem to matter. I let my head fall back on the seat and I shut my eyes. Her voice sounded far away. She was saying, "It's all right now. Just relax."

I don't know how long later it was when I opened my eyes. We were passing Bryant Park, going slow in heavy traffic. She was turned a little toward me in the far corner of the cab, studying me closely. There was a buzzing in my head and my neck hurt. I said the first thing that popped into my head. I said, "Did I mention that you've got lovely eyes?"

Her lips smiled, but her eyes didn't. She tossed her handkerchief on the floor of the cab. It was bloody.

"Your nose has stopped bleeding," she said.

I hadn't known my nose was bleeding and I hadn't felt her dabbing at me with her handkerchief. I said, "I must look a mess."

"Not so bad. A clean shirt and a wet rag for the lapels of your coat would fix you up."

I put my hand on the back of my neck and moved my head around, trying to take out the kink.

"That bartender's quite a hand at necking," I said.

The taxi stopped for a red light, and I fished around in my pockets for a cigarette, but couldn't find any. I must have left them on the bar with my drink. She opened her purse and gave me a Raleigh. Well, our brand of cigarettes was something we had in common, anyway. She held a match for me, and I lit up.

"Thanks." I took a couple of deep drags, and the smoke was good in my lungs. I said, "I'm sorry if I butted in at the wrong time, but ..."

"You were a lifesaver. I'm afraid I couldn't have handled him any longer."

"He did seem sort of annoyed."

"Distinctly," she said. She rubbed her cheek ruefully, but she needn't have. There wasn't a trace of the slap. It was a damned nice cheek with a dimple in it.

"Who was your pal, anyhow?" I asked. "He seemed sort of familiar, but I can't place him."

"You don't know him."

I bluffed. "I think I do. I get around a lot. Just can't place him."

"His name doesn't matter," she said with a that's-that tone. She was looking out of the window now as the cab crawled through the traffic. I was tempted to devil her for the name of the guy who'd slapped her and tried to shoot me, but I let it ride.

"You're the doctor," I said.

She turned to me, leaning forward, and she put her hand on my wrist. For a moment, there wasn't any mask over the blue eyes. They were serious, grateful, troubled. They were the bluest eyes I ever saw.

"It was swell of you," she said. "It was crazy, though. You'll be sorry for it."

"My venerable father tells me no gentleman ever regrets helping a lady in distress. That is, unless he puts it in writing."

"You don't understand. If he finds you …"

"He'll get another poke in the gob."

"Don't you see he'll kill you?"

"If I've got to be so afraid of him, why don't you tell me his name? Then I'll know who I've got to look out for."

She bit her lip and looked out the window. Her voice was very low.

"I can't," she said.

I wanted to ask her if the fellow with the gun was one of Nicky Pet's lugs, but I checked myself. It would be better to take things easy. So I went airy.

"Then let's forget him," I said. "I'm a lot more interested in us, anyhow."

She turned to me with one eyebrow lifted a bit. The mask had slipped over the blue eyes again.

"And what about us?" she said.

"Everything. Chiefly a drink. It seems to me this reunion calls for one."

"Reunion?"

"Surely you haven't forgotten our meeting on the train?"

She hesitated a moment. She was trying to calculate her smartest play. Then she shook her head. "Of course not," she said.

She waited for me to go on, waited for me to bring up our scuffle in the Wannermans' thicket, I guess, but I skipped it and talked about the necessity of celebrating our meeting with a drink for auld lang syne.

"After all," I said, "it isn't everybody who has a corpse in common."

She flinched at that, but came up smiling. "I suppose murder should constitute an introduction, after all," she said.

"Indubitably, madame. Where'll we go?"

"I'm sorry, Mister ..."

"Bixby," I said. "Tie Bixby."

"Oh, yes, I remember," she said. I knew damned well she remembered, but I didn't let on.

"I don't want to seem ungrateful," she said, "but I do have an appointment."

"Appointments were made to be broken."

"I can't," she said. "It's ... it's important. So if you're feeling all right, you can let me out at the corner."

"Sorry, but I refuse to be stuck for the cab. It's a principle."

"Then, I'll let you out."

"Nope. I refuse to let a lady give me a ride. It's another principle."

"What would you suggest?"

"I'd suggest Scotch and soda, but you can even have rye and ginger ale and I'll still think you've got lovely eyes."

She shook her head, smiling. "I have to keep this appointment."

"I'll have a relapse if you leave me."

She frowned. "Please, I do appreciate what you did, and I know you're trying to be kind, but I can't …"

"I think you can," I said. There wasn't any fun in my voice. "We've got a most interesting subject to discuss."

"Indeed?"

"Yep. Murder."

She didn't panic worth a damn. All she said was, coldly, "I told the police all I know about that, I'm afraid."

"There was another murder. You didn't tell them about that."

"Another?" The blue eyes widened, registering innocent surprise. If I hadn't had the red calot in my pocket, I might have been taken in by it.

"How could I tell them about something I didn't even know had happened?" she asked.

"I don't suppose you're interested in knowing who was killed, either?"

"Not especially. And I do have to keep my appointment. You'll have to let me out."

I didn't say anything. I drew the red calot out of my pocket and sat toying with it in an absent-minded sort of way.

"Somebody murdered Dirck Wannerman before he was burned," I said. "They shot an air bubble into a vein with a hypodermic needle. When the bubble reached his heart, he died."

She was dead white. Her hand trembled as she lit a cigarette. She looked out of the window a moment and then she turned quietly to me.

"It seems I'll take that Scotch, after all," she said.

So we went to the Pink Elephant bar at the Hotel Bristol in Forty-eighth Street. I cleaned up in the washroom and then we had some drinks. It always makes me feel better to see the dancing pink elephants behind the bar.

A dark guy came in and Gretchen smiled at him. He looked blank as though she'd made a mistake, but I figured that might be a stall for my benefit. I knew I was being a sap, but her smiling at the guy made me sore and I got sarcastic.

"Escorting you seems to come under the head of a hazardous occupation," I said. "I hope this friend of yours is less hostile than the last one."

"He's not a friend. He's an actor."

"You must be thinking of dramatic critics. I seem to remember hearing once about an actor who had a friend."

"He doesn't know me from Adam's off ox," she said. "I just smiled at him because he's a grand actor. I saw him in *The Paycock*."

It turned out the guy was Denis O'Dea, one of the Abbey Players. She thought they were swell.

"Well, don't worry about him not smiling back. Nobody's ever macadamized the course of true love."

"It's a waste of time for you to try to be a philosopher," she said. "You're much too sober."

"Sobriety's a malady for which, thank God, there's always an effective antidote."

So we had a couple of antidotes, talking about everything in the world except the one thing we both were thinking about, and after a long time our talk just dwindled off and we sat there silent. Both of us were nursing our drinks, each hoping the other would get tight and talk. Finally, I said, "We've wasted a lot of time."

She smiled wanly. "I am rather tired of sparring."

"All right, let's get down to business." I paused, trying to frame my first question, but she beat me to the draw.

"Just why did you get mixed up in this?" she asked.

"I thought I told you. Madame, I'm a gent. And what kind of a gent will go around seeing ladies get socked in the kisser?"

"I thought we were through sparring," she said. She leaned a little forward, tensely. "I want ... I've got to know where you fit into this ... this awful mess."

"I might ask you the same question," I said.

"We aren't getting very far, are we?"

"Why did you pretend you didn't know Mickey Carr?" I asked.

She looked blank, lifting an eyebrow questioningly, but I said, "It won't go, baby. He was the guy who got his throat cut on the train, and you know it as well as I do."

"If you know already, why ask me?" She sipped her drink as cool as cool. She could act, all right. She said, "But since you have asked me, I suppose I might as well tell you that you're crazy. I never saw him before in my life."

"I'm not crazy enough to believe you," I said.

"Do you really think insults are amusing, Mr. Bixby?"

"I ... Oh, damn it to hell! You knew Carr and I've got to know why you pretended you didn't. Listen, baby, you're just laying up trouble for yourself. You both worked at the Golden Mirror, and you're going to have a lot of explaining to do. Those cops won't be as easy as I am. They'll make you talk."

She sat for a moment silent, toying with her glass, and then she looked up and said quietly, "All right, I did know him. What next?"

"Why did you lie about it to Conners? Why were you two on the train pretending not to be together? Good Lord, don't you see you were talking yourself right into the clink?"

"I'm afraid I didn't act very bright."

"Maybe it's not too late," I said. "I want to help. I think …"

"You're very gallant."

"Nuts to that. Suppose you start telling me what you and Mickey Carr were going to Scrafton for?"

"I can't tell you." She wasn't melodramatic about it. She just said it. She meant it, too. I tried another angle.

"Maybe you can tell me what you were doing snooping around Wannerman's laboratory?"

"I can't tell you that, either."

"Can't?"

"Won't, then." She looked at me intently a few moments. Then she said, "Could I ask you a question?"

"Sure, fire away."

"Did you kill Mickey Carr?"

"Don't be a fool! Why should I have killed him!"

"That's what I'm trying to figure out," she said. "You could have killed him without anybody seeing you leave your seat."

It was stalemate. I said, "Well, since we both suspect each other, let's forget it and have a good time."

"In the hope that one of us will get tight enough to talk indiscreetly?"

"That's as good a reason as any, if you need a reason to get plastered. Personally, though, that crack of yours makes me suspect you're probably a barbarian. My sainted father says the mark of a barbarian is that he needs a reason to get drunk."

She reached impulsively across the table and gave my hand a little squeeze. "I think we could both use some fun," she said.

So we got a cab and I said, "Just drive around." The driver started for Central Park, but when he got to

Fifty-ninth Street, I told him to skip the park. I said, "Go anywhere except the park."

He thought I was a screwball, but he didn't say anything. New York hackies are used to screwballs. He swung up Fifth Avenue, and Gretchen asked me what was wrong with the park.

"Nothing, nothing at all," I said. "It's a very nice park, but everybody drives there."

"Everybody drives on Fifth Avenue, too."

"Don't be difficult, young woman." I was feeling crazy and I didn't give a damn. I said, "A fellow can ride through the park with any girl, but this is something special."

I expected a crack, but there wasn't any. I knew I was being forty kinds of a goggle-eyed sap, but it didn't seem to matter. I didn't give a damn if she had slit Mickey Carr's throat and killed Wannerman. At that moment, all I cared about was just to keep on riding with the girl beside me and never stop. It wasn't something I could explain to her, though. It's sort of hard to tell a woman you suspect of murder that you love her.

We rode a long time without talking, and when Gretchen finally spoke, her voice was sort of muffled. She said we'd better decide where we were going. "We can't ride around all day. You're spending a fortune."

"Okay," I said, "where do you want to go?"

"We could go to my place," she said.

"Don't be a dope. Don't you think your gun-toting pal will be laying for you there? And I have a chronic aversion to being shot. I'm funny that way."

"But I've got to go home some time."

"Not necessarily. You can hole up at my place."

She studied me silently, trying to figure my play. I said, "I don't have any etchings and my venerable father is a perfect chaperon."

"Thanks a lot, but I'll go to a hotel," she said. "Don't think I'm not grateful, but …"

"But you still suspect I've got an ax to grind."

"We both have," she said.

There wasn't anything I could say to that. She glanced at her wristwatch. It was five-thirty.

"He wouldn't dare do anything in daylight," she said. "If you don't mind, we'll go to my place and I'll pack a bag. Then I'll go to a hotel."

I told the driver to go to her house on Commerce Street, and she looked surprised. I said, "Sure, I know the number. I'm not a complete dope."

She was a fool to go back to her house, but if she wanted to, okay. I didn't give a hang.

I kept my weather eye open when we got to the Village and I took a good look around when the cab stopped in front of her house, but there was nary a sign of Tuck Waist or anybody else who looked suspicious. As we went up the stairs, she said, "I do appreciate your invitation, but I'll go to a hotel."

"That's all right with me. I may manage to survive without your charming company."

She started to say something, but didn't. She unlocked her door and stepped into a little foyer. I followed her and closed the door. She pushed back a blue drape and we stepped into the room. We stopped dead.

Tuck Waist was standing across the room and he had a gun.

Chapter Eight

Tuck Waist was smirking at us. "So you brought your boyfriend along," he said. "That's just ducky. It saves me the trouble of hunting him up."

The girl took an impulsive step forward, and the smirk froze. His voice crackled. "Stay where you are! I'll plug you if you move. Maybe I will, anyway, but we've got to have a little talk first."

"He didn't have anything to do with it, Tony." The girl's hands were clenched at her sides. "Honest, Tony, he just happened to be there."

"Now wouldn't I be a sap to believe that?"

"I swear it, Tony! Please ..."

"Button up your face! You tell me what I want to know and nothing else, see?"

He looked at me. "And you, big shot, you stay put, or I'll blow your guts out. I owe you one, anyhow. Now sit down, both of you."

We sat down on the studio couch, and the gunman let the muzzle of his pistol drop a little as he stood there across the room, but he was too far away to rush. He'd have shot us both before I could've taken a step.

"I want that dough," he said. "All of it."

The girl leaned forward. "I told you I didn't get it, Tony! We were on our way and Mickey was killed and ..."

"Don't try to play me for a sap. Cough it up."

"Good God, Tony, I haven't got it! I was going to get it, I swear I was, but the fire ..."

"Yeah, I read about it in the paper. But that stall don't go, sister."

"I wouldn't cross you, Tony. I swear I wouldn't."

"I know you won't. I won't let you."

"Can't you understand? When I saw Mickey was dead, I was scared. I was going through with it, but then I saw the place go up in fire, and I ran, and …"

"Figured you'd keep the dough for yourself. Well, you figured wrong."

"If I haven't got the money …"

"Then you'd better get it," he said. "And you'd better get it now. If you don't, you and your boyfriend can have a double funeral."

"Listen," I said. "I don't know what you two are talking about. I don't know about any money. But I know you'd be a sap to bump us off. They'd get you before you went a block."

"Yeah? Nobody saw me come down the fire escape and nobody'll see me go. They'll just find you two rats here. And you won't be able to tell nobody nothing."

The girl broke in. "If I'd got the money, I'd have split with you, Tony. I swear I would."

"You had your chance for a split, and there ain't going to be none now. I'm taking it all."

Her voice rose shrilly. "But I haven't got it! I tell you, Tony, I didn't get it!"

"You're a lying bitch!" His eyes were slits. Rage made the hand that held the gun tremble a little. He was about mad enough to shoot.

She stood up. "Tony, you've got to listen to me. I swear …"

His voice cut. It was icy: "You asked for it. You're going to get it. No dame's going to cross me."

"Oh, Tony …"

He glanced at me. "Stand up, sucker."

I stood up beside the girl. He said, "You first, big shot, then her. And it's going to hurt you a lot worse'n it'll hurt me."

My knees were shaking. So this was how it felt to die. I looked at the girl. I tried to smile, but I felt too sick. He was saying something to me. It seemed he was talking from a long way off.

"How'll you take it," he said, "in the belly or in the back?"

I knew he was going to shoot. I knew the only chance I had was to rush him. But I couldn't move. I couldn't even shut my eyes. I just stood there and stared at the gun pointing at me. I wondered if it would hurt to die. Then the girl spoke.

"You win, Tony. If you let us go, I'll give you the money."

"I thought you'd get smart," he said.

"You'll let us go if I give it to you?"

"Sure," he said. "Sure, I will."

I knew he was lying. I knew he'd murder us the moment he got his hands on the money. I wanted to tell her so, but I couldn't speak. Everything was tumbling around in my head.

"It's not here," she said. "I put it in a safety deposit box, but I'll get the key for you."

"Where is it?"

She shook her head. "I've got to have some guarantee you won't kill us after you get it."

"You've got to take a chance on that," he said. "You ain't in the driver's seat."

She glanced at me. "I guess we're licked, honey."

I gawked at her. She was making some play I couldn't follow. She said, "I guess we'll have to give it to him."

"I ... Yeah, sure," I said. I didn't know what the angle was, but I had to trail along.

"I'll get it," she said. She took a step forward and stopped, putting her hand to her forehead. She said,

"I ... I think I'm going to faint."

Before either of us could speak, she crumpled up on the floor. The gunman and I stood staring at her stupidly and then he said, "Snap out of it, sister! That stall won't do you any good!"

I started to pick her up, but he snapped, "Back, you!" He looked at the girl lying on the floor. He said, "Get up before I count three or I'll let your boyfriend have it. One ..."

She didn't stir. I said, "Can't you see she's really out?"

"Two ..."

The girl didn't move.

"Three!"

She just lay there. He said, "Your tough luck, big shot."

I tried to think of something to say, but I couldn't. I wished he'd shoot and get it over with. He glanced at the girl again and his gun wavered. He said, "I guess she ain't faking. Pick her up."

I hardly had strength enough to lift the girl, but I managed it. Twice I'd braced myself for the bullets, and twice he hadn't fired. My nerves were about to snap. I stumbled a little as I turned toward the couch to put the unconscious girl down on it. As I laid her down, my back blocking his view of her face, she opened her eyes. They were clear. She hadn't fainted at all. Her eyes were trying to tell me something.

As I straightened up, she closed her eyes. I fumbled in my head to try to understand what she wanted me to do. I turned to the gunman and said, "I better get some smelling salts." I started for the bathroom, but he stopped me.

"Never mind that," he said. "We'll stay right here."

I flared at him. "You don't want her to die, do you?

Damn it, you'll never find the safety deposit keys if she does. I don't know where she put 'em."

He bit his lip, doubtfully, angrily. He glanced around the room. A bottle half full of whiskey, a siphon and some glasses were on the bottom shelf of her bookcase. He grinned mockingly.

"Give her a snort of that," he said. "That'll bring the little tramp around."

I got the bottle and a glass and went over to the couch. It was one chance in a million, but I had to take it.

She stirred a little, moaned weakly. I poured a drink and put the bottle beside the couch. I lifted her with one arm and held the whiskey to her mouth.

"Drink it, baby. It'll do you good." I lifted the glass a little, and a few drops of whiskey trickled down her chin. She opened her eyes slowly. I said, "Drink it all."

The gunman spoke behind me. "Sure, and then get them keys, or I'll give you a slug."

She sat up and then she tried to stand, but she swayed feebly and sat down on the edge of the couch. It was a swell act.

"I'll be all right," she said. "Just a moment."

"Make it snappy, sister."

She looked up and he took a step toward her. She pleaded, "Just a second, Tony. Could I have another drink?"

He snapped impatiently, "Sure, sure, get a move on."

I picked up the bottle and the glass from the floor. At that moment she took a deep breath and said, "The keys are in that green bowl beside you."

He turned involuntarily. And in that split fraction of a second, I swung the bottle as a club on the pistol. The crack of the bottle and the shot were at the same moment. I grabbed his gun arm before he could fire again. He was cursing. He was pounding me with his free fist, but I hung on to his gun wrist with both hands. My knees were buckling. I sagged down. He kicked me from him as I slumped.

I was dimly conscious of him, dimly conscious he was going to shoot. I was lying on my back. I tried to lift myself. I had to get up. I had to get him. I wondered why he didn't shoot.

It happened quicker than a man can tell it. The aching fog cleared from my eyes. I saw the girl had grabbed his gun arm. He was smashing her with his other fist, but she hung on. She closed her teeth on his hand. He howled. The gun fell. His fist smashed her. She crashed onto the floor. She was sobbing. She was trying to reach the gun.

I stumbled up. He didn't have time to get the gun. But he kicked it from beneath her hand. The gun slid off under the couch. She was crawling and he kicked her. She lay there moaning. He whirled on me.

The bottle was lying on the floor as I got up. My hand closed on the neck. The bottom of the bottle was broken off. He rushed me.

I swung the jagged bottle into his face. He went back on his heels. He clapped his hands over his face and bent over. He was screaming.

I swung again. I was still clutching the broken stump of the bottle. The rest of it broke off against the side of his head. He fell over a chair. He was still screaming.

"I can't see … I can't see …"

It was dusky in the room now. The cops would be coming. People must have heard the noise. We had to get away. She was trying to get up and I helped her. He wasn't screaming now. He was hunched up on the floor with his bloody face in his hands. The last thing we heard was him moaning that he couldn't see.

A fat dame was standing in the hall when I flung the door open. She said, "What's wrong?"

I shoved her and she flopped down on the floor. Gretchen was behind me when we started down the stairs. Some people were on the second-floor landing and a guy said, "Wait till the police get here! You can't go!"

I let my fist fly. It smacked him on the nose. He banged back against the wall. He was yelling something, and a woman ran screaming down the stairs, but nobody tried to stop us. We hurried down. The woman ducked into an apartment and slammed the door. She was still screaming.

Gretchen grabbed my arm. "Slow down," she said. "You can't slug your way through seven million people."

So we stopped at the bottom of the stairs. Somebody was banging on the front door. That would be the cops. They'd be coming in. We were trapped.

There was only one chance for us. I flung my hat down the stairway to the basement. I snatched off her red calot and threw it after my hat.

"You don't know me," I said. "We're tenants. We're scared to death. Slip out right after me."

The woman in the apartment was still screaming. I guess everybody else was in the halls and so they didn't push the buzzer for the cop. The screaming woman was yelling too loud to hear him ringing. I ran to the front door. I threw it open. A couple of cops rushed in.

"Quick," I said. "He's killing her!"

They started up the stairs, and I yelled, "Top floor! The other one got away!"

I went on out the front door, but another cop was standing in the vestibule. He said, "What's your hurry?"

"He'll kill her!"

Gretchen was right behind me. "There were two of them," she said.

I was glad the vestibule was dim and he couldn't get a good look at her. I said, "Damned if I live in this house another night. I'm going to a hotel."

"You better wait," the cop said.

I said, "Just so they make it snappy."

Gretchen asked him something, and the cop turned to her. I let him have it. My fist caught him on the point of the jaw, just below the ear. He crashed down in the vestibule. He was dead to the world.

I pulled open the outer door, and Gretchen ran through. There were some people in the street and some were looking out of windows, but we didn't trouble with them.

"Walk fast, but don't run," I said.

Then I heard somebody yelling. I looked back. A cop was poking his head out of an upper window and yelling at us. A cab was pulled over to the curb and the driver was gawking. The people were looking at us.

I snatched open the cab door and we tumbled in. Something cracked. The cop was shooting at us from the window. The hackie looked around and his jaw was working, but no sound came. I stuck my hand inside my coat.

"Step on it!" I cried. "I'll bump you if they get us!"

He didn't stop to ask questions. The cop was shooting. I heard somebody yelling. The cab lurched away, swung down Hudson. A red light flashed on ahead of us.

"Don't stop, buddy!" I hoped my voice sounded like a killer's. It must have. He put on the gas at the corner, and I saw a truck swerve up on the sidewalk to keep from hitting us.

"If we get away, you won't get hurt," I said. "But I'll blow you to hell if we don't."

"I'm doing the best I can," he said. His voice was a croak.

"West here," I said, and he swung toward the river. I couldn't see anybody on the street. It was a block of warehouses.

"Hold it!"

He jammed on the brakes and turned around. "Please, mister, I ain't …"

"Nobody's going to get hurt if you keep your mouth buttoned."

His voice trembled. "I ain't saying a word, mister."

"Get out of the cab, and if you make a break for it, I'll blast you. And leave the motor running."

"Okay, mister, okay. I'm doing just what you say."

He got out of the cab, and I opened the door. I told Gretchen, "Keep this bastard covered."

"I got him," she said.

I got out and told him to walk into the shadow of the warehouse. I said, "Now let your pants down. Don't take 'em off. Just drop 'em around your feet."

He fumbled with his belt, and his trousers fell around his feet. It'd take him a few minutes to pull them up or kick out of 'em, and by that time we'd be long gone.

"You'll find your hack down at the Hudson Tubes," I said. "Sorry, buddy, but we got to get back to Jersey."

I snatched off his cap and put it on my head. It was too little, but that didn't matter. I ran back to the cab and got in the driver's seat. I pulled down the flag.

"Okay, lady," I said, and we rolled off. In the mirror I could see Gretchen leaning back nonchalantly, lighting a cigarette. If anybody noticed us, they saw only a girl without a trouble in the world and a hackie making an honest dime. I was doing some tall thinking, though, and I had my plan doped out by the time we turned up Hudson and stopped for a red light at Charles. It might not work, but it was the best chance for us. At least, I couldn't figure anything else as good. I half-turned to the girl.

"We've got five minutes, if we're lucky," I said. "I'll drop you at my place. Ring and go on up. Spill it all to my father and tell him I'll be back as soon as I can ditch this cab."

"They're liable to pick you up."

"They're a lot more liable to pick us both up if I leave it parked in front of my dump. And I'm safe once I get rid of this hot hack. Nobody at your place knows who I am. I don't think any of them would recognize me again, unless that taxi driver figures out that my squint-eye was a stall."

The traffic light went green, and we rolled on. A police radio car came zipping along. The cops didn't even glance at us as they whizzed by. We rode on to Jane, and I pulled up in front of my house.

"Make a stall of paying me," I said. "Just in case."

It was pretty dark now, and I didn't think anybody would notice us, but I didn't want to take any chances. All you need to flood Holland is just one little hole in the dikes.

She got out and extended her hand as though giving me my fare. I said, "Keep your chin up, baby."

I scrammed out of there with the cab as she turned toward the house. I had to make tracks. I figured they must have a radio alarm for the hack out by now. And the thought that at any moment a radio patrol was liable to spot the number didn't make me enjoy motoring any more.

I circled a little and then swung east into Twelfth Street, coming up behind Loew's Sheridan Theatre, and I pulled in to the curb. I got out and went down into the subway station. A fellow at the newsstand at the entrance looked at me sort of funny, but I didn't let him get a good look at my face. As I dropped my dime in the slot and went through the turnstile, I thought it was a lucky break that guy had noticed me ditch the cab. Now when the cops found the hack, they'd probably learn from the guy that the driver beat it by subway. I'd hoped my gag to the hackie that we had to make Jersey would put them off the track, but I wasn't banking on it. There seemed more chance this stall would go over. I ditched the stolen cap in a trash can and walked on along the subway platform to the Fourteenth Street exit. I went up to the street and walked east to Sixth Avenue. I wanted to take a cab here, but I couldn't risk it. The hackie might remember me. So I caught the elevated and got off at the Eighth Street station. Nobody paid any attention to my being bareheaded. Which was one of the benefits of the Village or a campus if you haven't got a hat.

I strolled over to the Eighth Street Playhouse and saw they were playing a revival of *The Gilded Lily*. That was a break for me. It was my alibi if I happened to need one. If the dumb cops or anybody came around asking where I'd been for the past two hours, I was in that movie. I'd seen the movie on its first run there, and I was willing to risk a grilling on it. I saw the doorman change the lobby clock to show that the short subjects were playing. I noted what they were from the billboard as people came out, but they weren't anything I'd ever seen. I had to take my chances on being questioned about them. I didn't think they could trip me up on the feature. After all, Claudette Colbert was in it. And the dope who'd forget Colbert deserved twenty to life.

The people were coming out of the theater, so I drifted in among them and hailed a cab at the curb. I gave him my address on Jane.

"That's a swell movie at the Eighth Street," I said. He said, "Yeah."

After that the conversation languished, and when he stopped at my house and I got out, I said, "I'm sorry, Jack, but I got to skunk you. I'll make it up some time."

He looked disgusted as I paid him the exact fare without a tip. He didn't say anything, but he looked plenty, and I gave him all the chance in the world to memorize my pan. I wanted to be sure he'd remember me if I had to have an alibi. As I went into the house and let myself in with my key, I mentally patted myself on the back. The hackie would remember me, but even a cop would see he wasn't trying to do me a favor by giving me an alibi. Which would be a lot more convincing than if he remembered me because I'd overtipped him.

When I opened the door to my apartment, Gretchen half rose from the couch, but Pa didn't budge. He barely glanced at me from the chair where he sat with his feet, as usual, stretched out in front of him.

The girl laughed nervously. "I thought you were Scotland Yard, at least."

"Your failure to knock was doubtless a very fine tribute to my venerable years," Pa said, "but it was a damnable insult to my manhood."

"I ditched the cab," I said. I didn't feel like exchanging bum aphorisms. "If they finally tumble and ask me about you, my story is that you left me to keep a date and I went to the movies. So it must have been your date who had the trouble at your house."

Her left eyebrow flicked upward as though surprised, as though suspecting that I was trying to get out from under.

"You can drop the airs, Duchess. I think you've got a lot of explaining to do."

"Miss Jones has told me what happened," Pa broke in. "Suppose we let the explanations wait until we aren't all sitting on top of a volcano. Personally, I have no desire to remain seated for the eruption."

Gretchen said, "I'm afraid I'll have to accept your son's invitation to visit you awhile, after all. I left my purse at home, and I rather suspect a trip back for it would endanger my health."

"You can't stay," Pa said. "The first thing you've got to do is get out of here."

The girl looked as though she'd been slapped in the face. Then she got up. "I'm sorry," she said. "I didn't mean to inconvenience you."

Pa snapped, "Don't be a fool, young woman. I was beginning to suspect that I'd found an exception to the rule that an attractive woman must be an idiot, but I seem to have been mistaken."

"If this amuses you …"

"Oh, sit down!" He glared at her, and she sat down, but her eyes were blazing.

"You might as well have left your forwarding address for the police as to stay here," Pa said. "The instant Rafe Conner reads the story about you in the papers, with even the description of Tie those morons will be able to give, he'll figure the chances are that Tie was your companion. At least, he'll think that chance is worth the gamble."

"But there must be thousands of men …"

Pa lifted his long, skinny hand impatiently. "Of

course, there are. But Rafe Conner already suspects Tie isn't exactly kosher, and he doesn't suspect the others who might fit his description. So Conner will hotfoot it here, with or without a batch of New York detectives."

The girl's eyes were afraid, but she managed a smile.

"I was being stupid," she said. "I'm sorry. I wouldn't get you two in trouble for anything."

Pa snorted. "I don't intend to let you," he said.

She bit her lip. His voice became kinder. He said, "Don't mind me. And don't worry about what you'll do. We'll figure out something. What you need now is a drink."

I poured one for Pa, and me, but the girl shook her head. Pa said, "It's purely medicinal, young woman. We've got to outthink a whole police department of sober men, and that's a task requiring the proper degree of inebriety."

So she had her drink, and we sat silent a few minutes, each of us thinking our own thoughts. I couldn't get rid of the suspicion that she was playing us for a couple of saps. It was all I could do to keep myself from putting the pressure on her to make her spill everything she knew. What was this money the gunman Tuck Waist thought she had? Or did she really have it? Was her stall that saved us a stall about everything except the money? If she had it, how did she get it? If she didn't have it, how was she supposed to get it? What deal was she in on with Tuck Waist and the late lamented Mickey Carr? The next thought made me go cold! Had this girl cut Carr's throat to get the money? But if she had, how had she got the Gurkha knife from our house? If she hadn't, who had taken the knife? And if Gretchen Jones wasn't the murderer ...

I jumped up. I couldn't stay put any longer. I wanted to shake the truth out of her. The girl looked at me questioningly, but Pa seemed to understand. I expected him to crack wise, but he didn't. He sort of smiled and said, "Take it easy, son. I think I've doped out something."

"Then for God's sake spill it!" My nerves were ready to snap. I got a cigarette, but I had a hard time lighting it. That's how bad I had the jitters. I was scared, sure, but that wasn't the half of it. What had me going was all those crazy questions I couldn't answer and the chance that this dame was stringing us along so we'd burn ourselves saving her chestnuts.

"You kids stay put while I make a phone call," Pa said. "Don't answer the bell, either."

He unwound his lanky frame from the chair and got his hat. I said, "The phone's in by the bed."

"Think I'll walk down to a drugstore," he said. "I wouldn't like the phone company to have a record that a call came from here to this number I'm going to call."

"Who're you calling?" I couldn't keep the edginess out of my voice.

"Keep your shirt on, son. I'll tell you later."

The girl had frozen as he walked to the door, his long legs shambling and his shoulders stooped, and she was staring at him now with suspicion naked in her eyes. God knows what she'd have done if she'd had a gun.

Pa paused a moment before he opened the door and looked at us, his eyes blinking brightly from the ambush of his shaggy brows. He seemed amused at something.

"You'd better have another drink," he said, "and Miss Jones had better get cleaned up. You two don't look in the proper frame of mind to appreciate a tête-à-tête."

He went out, and the girl tried to laugh. It was a short, nervous sound, and it broke off short. She tried to be flip about it, though.

"I think I will remove the scars of battle, if you'll excuse me."

"Go right ahead," I said. I wanted to add a dirty crack about locking up the knives until she'd gone, but I didn't. I knew I was being a saphead to get soft about her. A dame who takes murder in her stride isn't exactly type casting for the role of love's young dream. But there wasn't anything I could do about it except swear I'd break her neck before I let her know I was such a mush brain.

While Pa was gone and Gretchen was washing up, I tried to figure out who Pa was calling, but it wasn't any use. That made me still sorer, and I just grunted when Gretchen came back to the living room and tried to make some polite conversation. She pretended not to notice, though.

"This is the first chance I've really had to thank you," she said. "You saved me twice and …"

"Skip it," I said.

"I can't, Tie. You've got to know I think you've been … Oh, pretty damned grand!"

"Sure, with a brass band. And you're not so dusty yourself. It was your stall that saved your neck and, incidentally, my own."

"Please …"

"Oh, let's cut out the mutual admiration society. All this gab gives me a swift pain."

She stood a moment silent. I could feel the tenseness, but I didn't look at her. Then she, spoke very quietly.

"I'm sorry," she said, "but I am grateful."

"Okay, you're grateful. Gratitude is a very rare

emotion, composed 90 per cent of hope the same bait will hook the fish again."

I slumped down in my chair and didn't even look at her as I tried to think of anything in the world except the girl and those damning questions. I could feel her studying me closely. I wondered what she was trying to figure out. The chances were she was trying to calculate whether I'd keep on being a nice doggie and fetch. I was about to break loose and blaze at her when Pa came in. He had some magazines under his arm and a paper bag.

"It's all fixed," he said. "Miss Jones will hide out with an old friend of mine."

I got up and said I'd go get a cab, but Pa said, "Such stupidity is invariably inherited from the maternal side of the family. Pour me a drink and sit down."

I fixed a drink while he said, "Miss Jones, you will leave here by yourself and walk to Union Square. You will take the East Side subway to Grand Central and walk the rest of the way to the address I give you. Under no circumstances take a cab. Too many cab drivers want to get their pictures in the papers by recognizing somebody."

She nodded, and he went on, "You will carry these magazines and this paper bag. It contains a toothbrush, toothpaste and a few things, but I fondly hope it looks like a working girl's evening grocery order. If any police happen to notice you, I think the magazines and the bag may avert suspicion. I do not believe they are part of the usual impedimenta of fugitives."

He paused a moment, stretching out his legs as he settled more comfortably into the chair, and his eyes sank deep behind the tangled brows. The corners of his mouth twitched as though the old man was remembering something gay and laughing out of the years.

"The lady's name is Mrs. Bell," he said. "I knew her … well, years ago. You can trust her."

He gave her an address just off Park Avenue in the Fifties, and I lifted an eyebrow at him. I didn't know he still knew anybody in the money. Pa ignored me, though. The girl picked up a pencil off the table and was going to jot down the address, but he stopped her.

"You'll have to trust your memory," he said. "If by any chance you should be picked up, I could not have my friend's address found on you."

"Oh, of course not." She repeated the address. "I'll remember it."

I said, "I'll go with you."

"Chivalry," observed Pa, "is paresis of the logic."

The girl laughed. "Thanks," she told me, "but your father's right. They'll be looking for a couple, and a girl with magazines and a paper bag … why, they'd as soon suspect a nun."

I subsided. It was her funeral, and I told myself I didn't give a care whether she made it or not.

"Well," she said, "I guess I'd better get started, if you can lend me a nickel."

Pa gave her a bill and told her she could pay him back when her ship came in. She hesitated and then put out her hand to me.

"Good-bye," she said, "and thanks."

I shook hands, and then I remembered who Mrs. Bell was. Mamie Bell, by God! I couldn't help grinning. She frowned, miffed.

"I was just thinking about your hostess," I said.

"Mrs. Bell?" She looked quickly at Pa, but he was sitting with his head sunk forward on his chest and his lips pursed as though sunk in reverie. She turned back to me. "What about Mrs. Bell?"

"She was New York's most notorious woman until old age retired her. The biggest guys in the country have been scared ever since she was going to write a book."

She made herself laugh gaily, but the kid was scared. I felt ashamed, but instead of saying so, I remembered all those questions I couldn't answer and the suspicion and I snapped at her.

"Now that we've got a hideout for you, suppose you do a little helping. What was that money your pal we blinded talked about?"

She didn't answer. She stared at me with stricken eyes. She shook her head.

"We've got to know. If we're ..."

Pa broke in. "Let her be, son. I think we may safely assume that it was blackmail."

"Is that right?" I flung the words at her. "Or would you rather tell the police?"

"I can't tell you," she said. Her voice trembled a little. Before I could hammer at her again, Pa told me to sit down and shut up.

"I think we may assume also that the object of the blackmail was Mr. Wannerman," he said. "Now I think we've detained Miss Jones long enough."

She didn't budge, though. She just stared at him and then she said, "It's not true. I didn't say so."

"Of course not," Pa said. His voice was low, silky. He got up and slowly led her toward the door.

"By the way," he said, "you lived in California in 1935, didn't you?"

I thought the girl was going to faint.

"How did you know?" she said.

Chapter Nine

Gretchen tried her damnedest, but she couldn't get another thing out of Pa. He shooed her off to Mamie Bell's and told her to stay holed-up and keep her mouth shut, no matter what happened.

"If you don't hear from Tie or me, it'll be because it's not safe," he said. "And just remember this, young woman—if you try to bolt and go it on your own, you'll be toddling straight into a murder charge."

She nodded. "You're being more than kind and I ..."

"Wait until we're out of the woods for that," Pa said. "Tell Mamie I'll see her as soon as I can, and don't tell her anything else."

She looked so awful small and scared and alone that I felt like a crumb for not saying something to cheer her up, but I couldn't think of anything to say. My head was tumbling with this tangle of new angles: Blackmail ... California ... 1935 ... what did these have to do with a guy's throat getting slit in a women's washroom on a Long Island Railroad train in 1948? How did they tie up with Wannerman getting a bubble of air shot into his vein?

I tried to devil Pa into letting me in on what he knew, but he said, "I don't know a thing, son."

"You were giving a mighty good imitation of knowing everybody's family skeleton by his first name just now."

"That was only guessing, son. I'm surprised you didn't jump to the conclusion before I did. After all, we both had the same facts to work with, and you had them first."

"Cut the Sherlock Holmes act, will you? What's it

all about, anyhow?"

Pa shrugged and poured himself another drink. He slumped deeper into the chair as he sat studying the drink with a sort of sorrows-of-the-world-on-his-shoulders expression. At last, he sighed.

"It is," he observed, "a sad characteristic of the decadence of our civilization that memories are no longer used to remember. I suppose it is because we delude ourselves with the belief that we can take short cuts in education, in the development of the human mind. We take doses of culture in anthological capsules, and so we no longer give our memories the sound training one gets from careful study of, say, history. Now Gibbon …"

"Okay, okay," I said. I was impatient and didn't want to hear a dissertation on scholarship. "Let's get down to cases. What did you mean by that crack about blackmail? Who's blackmailing who? And how did you know Gretchen was in California in 1935? What difference does it make, anyhow, where she was thirteen years ago?"

"There are none so deaf as those who stop up their ears with impatience," Pa said.

"For God's sake," I blurted, "this is no time to be making epigrams. Leaving everything else aside, don't you realize Rafe Conner is sure to sic the New York cops on to me the minute he sees in the morning papers that the cops are after Gretchen and a guy who looks like me? And that hackie's liable to identify me."

"Naturally," Pa said, "but it never averts the inevitable to get into a dither about it. And the chances are we've got the rest of the night to work before your friend Conner does put them on your trail."

I jumped up. "Listen," I said, "I don't know what this

whole setup is about, but I know I didn't have anything to do with any part of it. And I know I'm getting squeezed into being the fall guy. Well, I'm getting out from under. I'm telling Rafe everything I know and ..."

"You're not telling anything!" Pa's voice was like a sock on the jaw. His eyes were shooting fire. I wanted to tell him to go soak his head, but I sort of wilted and sat down.

"You've apparently been too blind to see the pattern of these murders, but you've got to trail along," he said. His voice was flat, frigid, like a judge reading a sentence to hang.

"It's too late for you to do anything except play it out," he said. "Conner would never believe you if you tried to spill it all now. You've covered up too much. You've meddled too much. And even if he did, the New York cops would have you on felonious assault."

I made one last effort to argue. "It's a clear case of self-defense," I said. "No jury ..."

Pa lifted his hand impatiently. "You're being naïve," he said. "What if you did beat the assault charge? They'd still have you dead to rights for grand larceny and possibly kidnaping as well. You did steal the cab. You did kidnap the driver. And your flight with the Jones girl was hardly the action of an innocent man who had merely defended himself. You've waited too long to crawfish, Tie. Your time to get out from under was before you so chivalrously rescued Miss Jones."

He was right, of course. I said, "Okay, I guess I'm elected."

"I'm afraid your election is by a much larger plurality than you realize," Pa said. "I see why you did it, of course, but it was stupid to flip your hat down the stairs. The police are bound to find it and trace it to you. They won't need the hackman's identification."

That stopped me a moment, but then I remembered. I'd bought the hat six months before at a bargain shop in Brooklyn. I'd been over there on a date and I'd left my hat in a cab, so I dropped in the nearest shop and got one. There was no name taking or anything like that. I told Pa, and I said, "They'll have a fat chance tracing the hat to me."

"We may thank Providence for the luck of fools," he said. "You'd better get moving now."

"Move where? I'm going to get some sleep."

"You seem to forget that you have an appointment with Paula Wannerman."

Damned if I hadn't. But I was two hours late already. I said, "She won't be waiting this long and if she is, she can wait. I've had all I can take for one day."

I started for the bedroom, but Pa stood up and took my arm, stopping me.

"You've got to keep that date, Tie. Everything may depend on it."

"I don't see …"

"We haven't got time to treat your intellectual myopia now. You've got to see her. Tomorrow may be too late."

I tried to argue that I didn't want to risk a reunion with the bartender or any of Tuck Waist's pals by keeping my date at the Golden Mirror with Paula, but I might as well have tried to argue with a steamroller as Pa. The upshot of it was that I phoned the Golden Mirror and asked if Miss Wannerman was there.

The guy said, "I'll find out."

A few moments later she came to the phone.

She sounded about as friendly as a Nazi in a synagogue, but I didn't argue with her. I told her to meet me at Main Street cafe and we could talk in the garden.

"Try talking to yourself," she said.

"Go up MacDougal and you'll walk right into it at Eighth Street. I'll ..."

"Who the hell do you think you are? Casanova Romeo Gable? Listen, sonny, you may be the pride of the Bixbys, but you'll never get another chance to stand me up."

Pa must have doped out her reaction from my face. He whispered, "Get mysterious, you idiot."

So I dropped my voice; made it tense. "Things have been happening too fast," I said. "I've got to see you. It's life and death for both of us. It's about to blow wide open."

"What am I supposed to do, bust out crying?"

"You'll have damned good cause to cry if you don't meet me. When they get through with you ..."

"Who? What do you mean?"

Her voice sounded suddenly afraid, but I said only, "I'll tell you when I see you. I've found out plenty."

Her voice went hard again. "Well, peddle it somewhere else," she said. "I know all the answers a girl needs to know."

She banged up the receiver before I could reply, but I figured her curiosity would be bigger than her peeve.

"She's scared, too," I said. "I wonder what of?"

"You might try asking her."

"I think I will," I said. I hurried to the bedroom and changed my clothes, but I didn't take time to wash up. I got my other hat out of the closet and said, "Okay, Simon, your little Legree's on his way."

"Not so fast," Pa said. "Here's what you've got to do. Find out everything you can about Wannerman's past. What did he do before he started these experiments?

Who were his friends? What women were there in his life? And be sure to get a picture of him."

"What good will that do?"

"If his daughter doesn't recall who the photographer was, find out where he went to school and dig up his college annual. That'll be old, of course, but better than nothing."

"It sounds screwy to me," I said.

"That's only the half of it," Pa said, and for the first time I could ever remember Pa sounded tired with the tiredness of an old man. There didn't seem to be anything I could say to cheer him up, either. So I left him there, an old man slumped down in a chair, not even noticing that his whiskey glass was empty beside him.

Paula was waiting for me in the garden at the rear of the Main Street restaurant, but she wasn't enthusiastic about it. She was sitting at a table under a big beach umbrella, nursing a highball and her grouch. She was wearing another green dress, and what I'd thought about her looks the first time was only the half of it. She was the kind of dame that you merely have to see to realize what a wonderful invention sin is.

She looked at me as though I were something she'd found under a log. Her green eyes would have blistered a tombstone. I ordered a Scotch and soda and then tried smoothing her down with a few compliments, but my batting average was .000.

"Suppose you dispense with the overture and get on with the sensational explaining act," she said. "If it isn't better than you look, God help you."

"It's the city life that's made me old before my time," I said. I rubbed my jaw. I was wondering whether Tuck Waist had been blinded for life by the broken bottle; wondering whether he'd died, making me a murderer. But I tried to act as chipper as a sparrow in a wheat bin.

"You know," I said, "I was a beautiful baby before the New York tempo got me."

"I don't doubt you were the handsomest usher at your parents' wedding, too."

"Must you be so subtle?" I said. "You're so charming that it would be a pleasure to wring your neck."

Her voice went sugary. "That must be why we get on so well, you darling boy. We have so many mutual feelings."

"All right, all right, now that we've insulted each other, let's have another drink and call it quits."

"But I don't want to quit," she said. "The pleasure of telling off a dullard is the only compensation one has for his company."

"Must you be sophomoric?"

"Truth usually is," she said.

"We might get somewhere if you'd quit your bum imitation of a Noel Coward heroine. It's really not funny."

"You're breaking my heart, Toots."

"For God's sake, must you be a fourth-rate stock actress?"

"Is that what it is?" she said. She was wide-eyed and she fairly cooed. "I thought you'd recognize it."

She had me steamed up, all right. Who the hell was she that I should give a holy hoot what she said? She knew she had me riled, too. She was downright purring. Well, nuts to her.

I beckoned to the waiter and got up. "Nice to have seen you," I said, "and it'll be a lot nicer never to see you again."

I paid the check and went out, but I hadn't taken

three steps beyond the door before somebody caught my arm. It was Paula. She was smiling a sort of twisted smile and she held my arm as we walked on toward Sixth Avenue. She didn't say anything. I was still sore and finally I made my voice as nasty as I could and said, "Would you mind telling me to what I owe this unexpected privilege?"

"I'm sorry, Tie."

"I suppose that makes everything just hunky-dory."

"Let's not fuss, please."

"Whose idea was it in the first place?"

"I know I was acting like a bitch, but …"

"Okay, sister, suppose we let it go at that and call it quits. You go your way, and I think I may manage to keep from interfering with you."

"Please, Tie, can't you understand? I shouldn't have been that way, but …"

"But what?"

"Nothing," she said, and she kept her eyes down as we walked north up Sixth Avenue. We were just past Bigelow's pharmacy when she stopped short and half-pulled me around so we were face to face. She looked up at me and her eyes were blazing and full of tears at the same time. The words blurted out.

"I thought you were with somebody else and I hated your guts. I guess I was jealous."

"Say, are you a screwball?"

She laughed. "Maybe I am," she said. "Maybe it's your fatal charm."

"Well, you've got sort of indirect ways of showing affection."

"Stop nagging at me, can't you? I don't want to row! How many times do I have to tell you to get it through that thick head of yours?"

What the devil could you do with a dame like that?

I said, "Okay, let's have a drink and start all over."

We dropped in at Goody's, and I waved to Andy behind the bar, but went on back to one of the booths at the rear for our confab. We got our drinks and I raised my glass.

"To the start of a beautiful friendship," I said.

"I hope we both mean the same thing by friendship."

She was a knockout, sure, and I don't mind a little hanky panky, but I wasn't in the market just then. I knew I was being a sap to pass up the chance, but I had more important things on my mind. A couple of murders, for instance, and the short end of a fifty-to-one shot that before another night I'd be getting a working over from the cops.

"You're a swell-looking kid, and don't think I don't know it," I said, "but we've got more important things to attend to first."

"You're wrong, whatever they are. And you don't know how wrong."

"For the love of Mike, be serious, won't you?"

"That's what I'm being," she said. Her eyes were green slits.

"We haven't got time to play," I said. "That'll have to wait until …"

She flared at me. "Oh, don't be so damned pure! Your name's not Saint Anthony!"

I had a yen to bat her between the eyes. I said, "Can't you get it through that blonde head of yours that murder is a serious business?"

She was looking at her glass on the table, and she was a moment silent, toying with the glass. She looked up quickly.

"I know you killed him, but I don't care," she said. "I …"

She broke off with a nervous laugh. I just stared at

her. I was too flabbergasted to speak. Suddenly her hand closed tight on my wrist and she flared at me again.

"Do you have to have a blueprint?" she said. "God damn you, can't you see I love you?"

Chapter Ten

It was out of character for my father's son to ignore a hint from any woman under ninety, let alone a swell looking babe who offered affection on a silver platter, but this was one time I wasn't feeling like a Bixby. The realization that I had only a few hours at best before the cops would be on my tail for grand larceny, if not for murder as well, was hardly conducive to a feeling of emotional reciprocity. Anyhow, even though it was cockeyed, even though I was kicking myself for being such a stooge, the way I felt about Gretchen Jones would have made any other woman seem like an anti-climax. Even Lola Montez. A look at the blonde across the table was all I needed to know I was being the international free-for-all champion sap, but that's the way it was.

Still, I couldn't afford to make Paula sore. The old gag about the fury of a woman scorned is a rank understatement, and I had to use Paula. I had to get her on our side for keeps and yet not let her know too much. So I had to do myself a fancy job of tightrope walking and no mistake. And the walking wasn't made any easier by the uncomfortable knowledge that one misstep would topple me for a harder fall than Niagara.

"You're a grand kid," I said. "I think you're swell, but ..."

"But you want me for a sister?"

"I didn't say that, baby. We won't get anywhere if you keep on putting words into my mouth."

"It doesn't seem to me we were getting places, anyway," she said. "I announce I love you, and you go coy on me, and there we've stuck."

"You're getting me all wrong, baby."

She smiled wryly. "I don't seem to be getting you any way," she said. "Let's have another drink to our stalemate."

I ordered another round and looked at her leaning a little toward me across the table, her green eyes misted over and her mouth a little parted.

"Gee, baby, you're tops," I said.

"But you don't aspire to such heights?"

"It's nothing like that," I said. "Can't you see I'm about to go nuts on this thing? I've got to get this mess straightened out before I can think of anything else. Then we can have some fine times."

"Are you offering me a bribe to be your ally?"

"Oh, hell, baby, I'm just telling you how things stack up. Look here: A man's throat is cut on a train. Then your father is killed and his body is burned. Don't you see I've got to clear up those murders before I can even turn around?"

I floundered for an explanation, but I knew as well as I knew water's wet that she wasn't swallowing my cock-and-bull story about being up to my neck in the murders because I was Rafe Conner's bosom pal and had to help him out.

"You ought to let Mr. Conner know you're helping him," she said. "It would save him a lot of work."

"What are you driving at?"

"He doesn't seem to know that you're giving him all this valuable assistance. I think he even suspects you of having some ulterior motive."

"What do you mean, ulterior motive?"

"You surely don't mean that he didn't tell you? Why, how could such allies as you and your friend Rafe Conner hold out on each other?"

"This isn't any time for guessing games. Would I be asking you if Rafe had told me?"

"My, my, isn't that disillusioning! Imagine Damon holding out on his beloved Pythias!"

She was smiling, a mocking smile, but there wasn't any mirth in it. Her green eyes were sharp, suspicious, trying to catch in my face some hint of what was going through my head.

I leaned back and took a drink. I said, "Go ahead if it amuses you. Just let me know when you're through clowning."

"I'm not amused by your lies, either," she snapped. She was leaning toward me. Her face was dead white. She bit her lip, looking at me as though she wanted to smash my face, and then she spat the words at me.

"You must think I'm a fool," she said. "You expect me to believe your interest in my father's murder is because of your deep friendship for a detective you knew when you were a boy. Oh, yes, he told me he'd known you. He wanted to know what dealings you had with father. I told him none that I knew of, but he wasn't convinced."

"I take it that was while I was hiding in your bedroom closet?"

"If you must be precise, I think you'd already got out of the house. You should have stopped to eavesdrop, though. You'd have found our discussion most entertaining."

"Sorry I missed it, but I had to hurry home to father. He worries so about me."

"You really should control your better instincts," she

said. "If you had, you'd have learned that your dear old pal suspects you murdered my father."

I froze. "He told you that?"

"He didn't have to. It was plain as day. And he'll do more than suspect you if I ever tell him what I know. He'll know…"

"Will you listen to me a minute? I don't know what you've got on your mind, but it's cockeyed. That's the second time you've said you know something that makes you think I killed your father."

"Not something I think," she said. "Something I know."

"Suppose you tell me what it is. I'd like to be in on the secret."

"Skip it," she said.

"If you're so sure I was the murderer, why did you warn me I'd be murdered if I didn't take a runout powder?"

"Nicky Pet," she said. "My hunch was that you were bucking him. Now I don't know." She fell silent, frowning a moment, before she went on. "I know I'm being crazy, but I can't help it, Tie. I don't care what you've done, don't care if you did kill him, I love you and I can't help myself. Sometimes I hate you for it, but I can't stop."

"Gee, baby, really …"

Her eyes were narrow now and her voice was cold. "I love you so damned much I'll kill you before I let another woman get you," she said. "I'll send you to the electric chair first."

"If you'd only tell me where you got this crazy idea I had something to do with killing your father …"

"How do you know the murder on the train was mixed up with his death if you didn't have something to do with it?"

"I don't know it. I swear …"

"You're a bum liar. You tied them in together yourself less than ten minutes ago when you were telling me why you had to be so pure."

"Call it guess work," I said. "I tell you I didn't have a thing to do with murdering anybody and I don't know what makes you think I did."

"Why don't you ask the girl in the red hat? I'm sure she could tell you."

I stared at her with my mouth open. How did she know about Gretchen? What did she know that made her tie me up with Gretchen? I tried to laugh it off, but I knew my flabbergasted face had been a dead giveaway that her crack had hit home. I had to cover up fast. And I had to find out what she knew before she started shooting off her mouth to Rafe. "Suppose we start at the beginning," I said. "Let's put all our cards on the table and then we'll know where we stand."

"All right," she said. "Start putting."

"You won't believe it, of course, but the straight truth is I got mixed up in these murders by accident, and Pa and I are trying to solve them because there's liable to be a reward from the insurance company. He's a nut on detective stuff, anyhow."

"Don't let my blonde hair deceive you," she said. "There's a limit even to a blonde's dumbness."

I tried a long bluff. It had worked when I wasn't bluffing and maybe it would now. I leaned back with a dead pan and motioned to the waiter for a check.

"Let's understand each other," I said. "There are a lot of angles about you that need explaining. Why were you glad your father was killed, for instance? Why weren't you surprised? What did your mother mean by saying *they* had killed him? Who are *they*?

Why should *they* kill him?"

She didn't answer. She sat staring at the fingers of her right hand drumming nervously on the table. I took a sip of my drink.

"I wondered about those things and a lot of others," I said, "but I was willing to gamble on you being on the up-and-up. I figured we could make a team and solve this mess. Sorry I was mistaken. We'll just call it quits."

I paid the check and lifted my glass to finish my drink. I even managed a remote smile.

"No hard feelings," I said. "Here's looking at you."

She didn't drink with me. She sat a moment longer staring at her slowly drumming fingers and then she laughed brittlely. She looked up and her green eyes were misted over.

"You're a devil," she said. "You know damned well I won't let you go."

I leaned forward. "That's the ticket, baby. We'll straighten this out. First off, I swear I didn't have anything to do with your father's death. Or the murder on the train, either. You believe that, don't you?"

She spoke quietly. Her voice was level, matter-of-fact. "No," she said.

I leaned forward. "Damn it, baby, what's eating you? What's given you this screwy notion that I killed somebody?"

"I saw you," she said.

I goggled at her. I had a sinking feeling in my stomach as I thought where a crack like that to Rafe Conner would leave me.

"I suppose you told the cops?"

She shook her head. "I wanted to hear what you had to say first. And to see how you acted."

"Gee, baby, you've got me on the ropes. You want me

to explain something I don't even know about. Back up and start over. Where did you see me that makes you so sure I did a job of murder?"

She sucked in her lower lip with momentary impatience. "If you insist on being humored," she said, "I saw you leaving my father's laboratory just before the fire."

"God damn it, you couldn't have seen me! I wasn't there!"

She was looking at me steadily. "Oh, I didn't see your face. It was too dark. I was sitting where you found me later, at the French doors in the living room, and I saw the lab door open and somebody come out. A man. He ran bent over a little and disappeared into that clump of shrubbery."

"But, baby, if you didn't see his face, how do you know that man was me?"

"It was you or an accomplice," she said. "Just after he disappeared, the fire started. The first blast lit up the lawn and I saw ... the other person and ..."

"What other person?"

She didn't seem to hear. She was leaning forward and her eyes never wavered from my face.

"The other person turned back into the thicket. I heard people yelling and saw my mother run out of the house. Oh, I know I was tight, tight enough not to care whether school kept or not, but I wasn't too tight to see. And I saw you come out of the thicket and run over to the crowd at the fire. I could see your face this time."

I tried to sound unimpressed: "Very neat, but it doesn't hold water."

"I'm afraid it does," she said. "A great deal of hot water—and you're in it."

"Don't be a sap. Look here. You see somebody run

away from the lab, but you don't see his face. Then you see somebody else standing there and that one beats it, too. Then you see me arrive. Which doesn't mean I was either one of the other fellows. Or maybe you think I was both of them?"

"The first person I saw ran into the thicket. So did the second person. Then you came out."

"Good Lord, what of that?"

"That thicket's not as big as the Everglades. It isn't likely you could come through it without meeting those others."

I tried to pooh-pooh, but she went right ahead in a chill, remote voice.

"So it adds up to one of two things," she said. "You were the man I saw running away or …"

"Just a second, baby! When the fire started, I was upstairs in my house with my family and Ruth Overhart."

"How convenient."

"Well, it's an airtight alibi," I said. "I couldn't be in two places at once, could I?"

"Then, why didn't you tell the police who it was you met in the thicket?"

"I didn't say I'd met …"

"You don't have to say. Two people were escaping through that thicket when you came through it from the other side. Oh, I'm granting your alibi will stand up. Now even if you did miss one of them, which isn't likely, you couldn't have missed both. And why would you keep secret from the police that you'd met somebody running away from the scene of the crime if you weren't an accomplice?"

"You're off your conk, baby. It was dark and anybody might …"

"Who was the girl in the red hat?" she snapped. I

tried to play dumb bunny, but I had the uneasy feeling that my face was a dead giveaway.

"Say, quit playing Mrs. Charlie Chan, will you? What girl do you mean?"

"The girl was the second person I saw run into that thicket. Who was she?"

"Search me," I said. "Listen, can't you get it through your head that I didn't meet anybody?"

The green eyes were studying me searchingly, and I took a swig of my drink.

"Now that's settled," I said, "what next?"

"It's a long way from settled. I think you're lying. I think you met someone in the thicket and kept it quiet. I want to know why."

"How many times do I have to tell you ..."

"Would you rather tell me or the police? Even if all you say was the truth, it won't do you any good."

I tried to bluff, saying she didn't know evidence from fairy tales, but it didn't work.

"Suppose what I saw is just circumstantial evidence," she said. "If I spill it to your friend Conner, it'll be strong enough to tie up the whole mystery in a neat little bundle with your name on it."

I knew she was right. And even if I could talk my way out of it, Gretchen couldn't. He'd spot the angle of the woman in the red hat right off the bat. Not that she wasn't in deep enough already with the New York cops after her for what we'd done to Tuck Waist.

By God! Tuck Waist! Guessing he was the man would make it all fit. He and Gretchen were in on something. The best guess seemed to be Pa's: they were blackmailing Wannerman and he made a row and they killed him and rigged up the fire hoping it would look like an accident. That was the only theory that did seem to fit, too. Of course, the first guess that

Wannerman had framed the fire and got caught in it was out. A man doesn't commit arson and shoot a bubble into himself.

Hold on, though. Suppose it wasn't blackmail. Suppose Gretchen, Tuck Waist, Fish Eye and Wannerman were in on a deal to burn the lab. Leave out his lack of motive for the moment. Suppose he had one we didn't know. They have a row and one of them slits Fish Eye's throat on the train. Then Tuck Waist kills Wannerman.

Or suppose Nicky Pet was the answer. He was suspicious Wannerman was holding out on him and he'd started getting tough about it. But would he have had Wannerman bumped off before his mouthpiece had that showdown with him? Maybe that's just what he would have done. Maybe that date was just to throw off suspicion. A hypodermic and a fake fire weren't like Nicky Pet's usual murders, but that may have been the reason it was done that way. And there was motive enough if Nicky Pet was sure Wannerman was trying to double-cross him and delay until he could sell his process to a silk company and pocket the dough himself. Hell, yes, for the shyster Sally had let it slip that they thought Wannerman's insurance was made out to them to protect Nicky's investment. It was beginning to add up.

I looked quickly at the girl and asked, "When your mother said *they* killed your father, she meant Nicky Pet's crowd, didn't she?"

"I wondered how long it'd be before you remembered I was here," she said. "Your guess is right. She saw a picture of Nicky Pet in a newspaper and recognized him as father's backer, and ever since then she'd been frightened. She begged father to get out of it, but he told her to mind her business. What he got served him right."

"It seems to me the police might wonder why you hated your father so much."

"Let 'em wonder!" Her eyes blazed. "He was a filthy beast. He wrecked my mother's life, and he tried to put mine in a straitjacket, but I wouldn't let him."

"That sounds like a bum second act ending."

"Reality usually does," she said.

"Sorry. Go ahead."

She hesitated. Then she blurted the words defiantly.

"Why not? Ruth's a fool to think we could keep it quiet. My father had been having an affair with Stella Vardis for four years, and mother found it out. I … I told her. Stella sang at the Golden Mirror. That's why I wanted to go there tonight. I learned about her and the next time my father started laying down the law to me, telling me I'd have to give up my sinful career, I fired out at him about Stella. Mother heard me, and that smashed everything for her."

"How did you find out about this mistress?"

"Oh, we met at the hairdresser's, and one day he came to call for her there. And I saw him through a curtain."

"Why didn't your mother leave him then?"

"I tried to make her, especially when he said he wouldn't give up Stella no matter what mother did. But she wouldn't. She worshipped him."

"Maybe enough to kill him?"

She flushed angrily. "Yes," she said, "but she didn't."

I was wondering how well Gretchen Jones had known Stella Vardis at the Golden Mirror, but all I said was: "What about this Vardis dame? What do you know about her outside of the fact she was your father's girlfriend?"

"Oh, Stella's all right. Just a girl on the make."

"Using your father for what she could get out of it?"

"That's what it was at first, I think, but later ... I don't know, Tie. I think she fell for him."

"The cleansing flame of love, no doubt?"

"It can work that way. I know Stella wasn't getting anything out of him, nothing to what she could have gotten if she'd taken some of the other chances she had, but she stuck to him. Even when mother went to her and said she'd never give father a divorce, Stella stuck. She was rather grand about it. She said she wanted him and not a wedding certificate."

"Where's she now?"

"I guess she's still living in Fifty-third Street. I went there a few times. I don't know what she's doing. She left the Golden Mirror about a month ago."

"Didn't it seem a little strange to you to be so palsy with your father's mistress?"

"We weren't chummy. We both went to Charmaine's and after we met, she'd ask me to stop at her place for a drink. To try to pump me about home, I guess, and there was just enough devil in me to enjoy playing dumb and telling her nothing."

"Who's Charmaine?"

"She's fat, fifty and a hairdresser. Stella has bleached hair and has to get it touched up every week or ten days, and she's always said the only person in town who did it properly was Charmaine. It was a phobia with her."

"When did you last see Vardis?"

"Oh, I don't know exactly. About the time she left the Golden Mirror. I bumped into her at Charmaine's, and she either said she'd quit show business or was going to quit. She said she was going to get married."

"Who'd she say the guy was?"

"She didn't. I don't think there was any. I think it

was just a stall to make me think she and my father were washed up. She must have suspected I knew about them after mother had the showdown with her."

"How do you know they weren't washed up?"

"I don't, but father told mother he'd broken with Stella, so I felt sure it was just a gag. If he'd really busted it up, I'd give odds he wouldn't have told mother. He'd rather have watched her suffer."

"That sounds pretty far-fetched."

"Not if you'd seen him. He was rotten clear through. Sometimes ... sometimes being his daughter makes me afraid what I may do."

She looked so pale and small and miserable, sitting there looking at her hands limp beside her highball glass, that I reached over and gave her right hand a squeeze. She looked up, and smiled a little.

"To what do I owe the demonstration of affection?" she asked.

"I was just thinking," I said. I felt like a heel, but it seemed my best play. "You're pretty swell, you know, and I was thinking what a celebration we'll have when is all cleared up."

"You don't mean Sir Galahad's melting?"

"He's melted," I said. "Any man who wasn't blind would be crazy about you."

"Especially if he thinks that's the way to keep my mouth shut."

"Oh, don't start the bitter-as-gall act again. I'm giving it to you straight. If you want to tell Rafe ..."

"Don't worry," she said. "I think you know who killed my father, but I don't care. I'm on your side, Tie, but God help you if you ever look at another woman."

"What's the use of all these melodramatics?"

Her hand froze on my wrist. She spoke so quietly it was difficult to hear her.

"If you go for another woman, I'll kill you," she said.

I tried to pass it off, but Paula was dead serious. I couldn't let myself think about Gretchen just then. That wasn't a time to wonder how I'd get out of being killed when Paula found out the real setup. I needed Paula and I had to use her, so I said we ought to celebrate our alliance by going uptown. On the way up in a cab, I asked her about a picture of her father. She said there weren't any. He'd never liked pictures and he'd torn up the few snapshots they had years before.

"He wouldn't even let mother keep his wedding picture," she said.

"There's bound to be one in his college annual, though. Where'd he go?"

She knew the school, but she didn't know what year he'd been graduated. I reflected it was lucky that it was a big eastern university, seeing the need we had for speed, but I didn't mention this to her. I started talking about us and I kissed her a few times in the cab, but finally she drew away and sank back in the opposite corner. She lit a cigarette.

"I think we'll skip the kissing until you can put your heart into your work," she said.

I remembered my hunch that Ruth and Paula had quarreled while I was out of the living room at the Wannerman house, and I tried to pump her about it without letting her know what I wanted. But she laughed at me.

"You needn't waste the major strategy," she said. "We had a row because Ruth wanted to tell the police about Stella. She said they had a right to know what mother meant by saying *they* killed father, too. But I couldn't see it. Mother's had enough hell without having her pride broken in public, too."

"Just where did Ruth fit in? I mean, what was her angle?"

"Oh, she's one of these do-your-duty-though-the-heavens-fall sort of women. She thought it was her duty."

"How'd she know about the Vardis affair?"

"Mother told her, I suppose. Mother depends a lot on Ruth. I think she's a sanctimonious dope, but mother gets a lot of comfort out of her. I know she told mother that she needn't worry about Stella any more after father said they'd broken up, and mother was sap enough to believe her."

"Well, it made her happy, didn't it, and didn't hurt her?"

"I suppose so. Oh, I know I'm unfair to Ruth. She means well. She's just so damnably proper. She never has approved of me."

"What about her and your father?"

"Nothing like that. I think she was nutty about him, but she's the type who'd never do anything about it."

We stopped at a couple of places and then, maybe an hour or so later, I decided it would be a smart thing to descend upon Stella Vardis at four o'clock in the morning and see how she was taking her ex-boyfriend's death. I tried to make Paula go to a hotel or go to the station to wait for a train home, but she wouldn't. I argued with her, but it didn't do any good. She curled up on the seat and blew smoke in my face.

"When I'm not with my Boy Scout, I feel so talkative I'm tempted to tell everything I know," she said.

So we wound up at Stella's apartment house together and found the hallboy asleep on three chairs pushed together in the lobby.

"Vardis?" he said, yawning, blinking at us sourly. "She don't live here no more."

He didn't enjoy waking up and it took all of Paula's wheedling and a five spot from me to make him remember anything else. He finally did remember, though.

"I guess you're friends of hers?" he said, eyeing Paula.

"I'm her cousin, and I've got to find her," she said, looking breathless. She'd have melted Patience's monument, and the hallboy was no monument.

"Well, lady, I guess it won't hurt to tell you, but don't ever let on where you got it. It'd be my neck. "

"Of course not," she said.

"Well," he said, "she left a couple of days ago, all of a sudden. It was early evening. I'd just come on, but Mr. Bosch hadn't left the office yet. Mr. Bosch stays till about seven mostly and…"

"Where did she say she was going?"

"That's what I'm trying to tell you, lady. She didn't say. I was standing at the door of Mr. Bosch's office over there and Miss Vardis said she had to leave right away. She paid up a couple of months' rent in advance and said she'd send back for her stuff then and sublet the apartment. Then she run out, but she didn't get a taxi. She walked off fast and kind of nervous. I thought it was kind of funny—she was leaving for two months and just carried a little overnight bag. Not much bigger'n a lunch box."

"Didn't she leave any forwarding address for mail, any address where you could reach her?"

"Nope, lady, all she said was she was going to get married."

We couldn't get any more out of him, so we went out and got in a taxi. I said, "It looks like Stella's reformation was on the level."

"It looks that way, but I don't know," she said. "I know enough about blondes to suspect them all.

Maybe because I'm one."

"Well, that winds it up for tonight, anyhow. Do you want to go to the station or a hotel?"

She was silent a moment. She lit a cigarette and blew a gust of smoke toward the roof of the cab.

"Couldn't we go to your place?" she said. "We could get some eggs and I could cook breakfast."

"Gee, baby, that'd be swell, but we can't." I hoped I sounded burdened with regret. I said, "My old man's holed up with me and he'd raise hell. He's been sick and he's sort of cranky. He'll be gone in a couple of days, though, and we'll get together for a real blowout."

She looked at me strangely a moment and then she laughed. It sounded strained. It was as mirthless as dying. Her voice was brittle.

"Honor thy father and mother—and miss opportunity's knock."

"What hotel do you want to go to?"

She became casual again. "Make it the Pennsylvania Station," she said. "I think I'd better go home."

While we were waiting at the Long Island Railroad gates for her train, I remembered something.

"By the way," I said, "you used to live in California, didn't you?"

"Yes, why?"

"In 1935?"

She hesitated. Then she said, "We lived in San Francisco that year, I think. What are you getting at?"

"I was just wondering," I said, but I knew she didn't believe me. I was trying to think of a stall if she pressed me, but my head was buzzing with what I'd learned and I couldn't. It was lucky they opened the gate just then.

We started toward the gate. She was saying something, but I wasn't listening. I was remembering

Pa's crack to Gretchen. She'd lived in California in 1935. She got scared to death when Pa asked her. Wannerman had lived in California in 1935, too. So had his wife and Paula. What had happened in California in 1935 that was important in a murder on Long Island in 1948?

We stopped at the gate. Paula was looking up at me, and I figured a kiss was indicated, but she turned her head a little and I only pecked her cheek.

"Thanks," she said, "but no charity."

"Don't be like that, baby."

"Let's wait until the time comes," she said. "You can tell your scoutmaster you've been a very good Boy Scout."

She was smiling as she started to go, but the smile faded. She turned back to me and put her hand tensely on my arm. She looked up at me steadily a moment before she hurried on to the train. All she said was:

"Remember this, Boy Scout, you can write your own ticket with me about everything except one. If ever you go for another woman, I'll kill you."

Chapter Eleven

I bought all the morning papers and taxied down to Riker's, the one on Eighth Street near George Kirk's Chelsea Bookshop. While I wrapped myself around ham and eggs, toast and a flock of coffees, I read what the papers had to say about the murders and our row on Commerce Street.

I picked up the *News* first and got a jolt that made my coffee go down the wrong pipe. When I got through spluttering, I turned to page three again. I'd been right the first time. Gretchen's picture was plastered all over the page with a caption that she was being sought for questioning by the police. They must have got the picture from the Golden Mirror's press agent.

The story said the cops wanted to question her and an unidentified man who fled in a stolen taxi after beating up Anthony Bonoramo in her flat. The cops had pegged her as a witness in the murder on the train and wanted to find out if there was any connection between that killing and the fight on Commerce Street. They also wanted her and the unidentified man on charges of felonious assault and grand larceny.

The paper said Bonoramo—I still thought Tuck Waist was a better name for him—had a police record of seven arrests and a couple of convictions for rolling a lush. The doctors said he was cut up pretty badly on the face and head, but they could save his sight and he was going to live. Which was lucky for us. They wouldn't get us on a murder rap, anyhow. Or maybe they would. There were still those two murders on Long Island. It was a break for us that Tuck Waist hadn't talked. At least, all the papers said he had refused to explain how he got mangled or name his assailants, and I guessed that was straight. After all, if he ratted on us, Gretchen was liable to rat on him. And if Pa was right. that would have plunked a shakedown rap right in his lap.

There didn't seem to be anything new on the murders. Grace Robinson came out flatly in the *News* that the police were convinced the killing on the train and Wannerman's death were part of the same scenario. The other papers hedged on it, saying the police and the D.A. were investigating the possibility of a connection. As far as the papers showed, Rafe Conner was keeping his trap shut about whatever he knew and the D.A., who didn't seem to know anything, was shooting off his face all over the landscape.

I pushed the papers aside and got another cup of coffee. This break called for a change of plans. We'd gambled that Rafe wouldn't get on my tail until he read the morning papers, but now it seems the cops had tumbled right off the bat to Gretchen being the girl in the smoker when Fish Eye was killed. That meant they must have phoned Rafe hours ago and the chances were he was already in New York. And I couldn't chance meeting him. I couldn't risk having that taxi driver identify me as the lug who stole his cab. I didn't have much fear the cop I'd slugged or the dopes in the hall would be able to swear to my identity, but the hackman was another matter.

Well, it was lucky I'd stopped off to read the papers before I went barging into my dump and, probably, the waiting arms of Rafe Conner or some New York dicks he'd tipped off. A little telephonic scouting seemed to be very much in order. So I paid my check and went to a phone booth in an all-night drugstore across the street. I heard the click as the phone was lifted from the hook in my flat. A man's voice was saying faintly, "I won't warn him." An instant later, louder now, the voice said, "Hello?" It was Pa's voice.

In that second, faster than the telling takes, I tumbled to what was up. Somebody was in the flat with Pa. He'd spoken to that somebody just as he lifted the phone from the hook to warn me, if it was me calling. His voice had been faint because he'd spoken before he raised the phone so the person—or persons—wouldn't suspect it was a warning. His voice was louder when he said "hello" because in that fragment of a second he'd raised the phone to his mouth. And the chances were whoever was there—

Rafe and probably the New York cops, too—was standing close enough to him to hear what I said. I snapped up the cue.

I said, "Tie?"

"No, he's not here," Pa said. I knew he recognized my voice, though. He said, "This is his father."

"Oh, hello, Mr. Bixby. This is Joe Thomas. I didn't know you were in town."

"Hello, Joe. I'm just here for a couple of days."

"It's a hell of a time to call up, Mr. Bixby, but I just got to town for the day and thought I might rout Tie out for breakfast. Do you know where I could get him?"

"Off on a toot, I guess. He hasn't been in all night. You might try ringing the bells of all the bars in town. He had that look in his eye when he left."

"Still the same old Tie. I thought he'd be settled down by this time."

"Where'll you be stopping? I'll tell him to ring you if he comes in."

"I haven't decided yet. I'll only be here until tonight."

"Try the Belmont. I can recommend the bar."

"I may do that. Thanks. Tell Tie I called, will you? I'll phone him later."

"If you get down this way, just ring the bell and come on up. I'm sitting here with a lonesome quart. But don't come too early, Joe, because I'm an old fellow now and I've got to have my sleep."

I hung up and went out to the corner and lit a cigarette. Pa had been trying to tell me something besides the fact that somebody was with him and for me to lay low. And it was so simple that I felt like a dope for not getting it on his first crack. There couldn't be any doubt about it: *ringing the bells of all the bars in town ... ring you ... Belmont ... ring the bell ...*

I flagged a taxi and rode uptown. I paid him off and

walked east. I hoped Pa had had a chance to pave the way for me, but I knew what he'd been trying to tell me, anyhow. He wanted me to take cover at Mamie Bell's.

I was within a block of the house before I remembered something else. I stopped dead. What a dope I was. Pa told "Joe Thomas" not to come to see him too early because he had to have his sleep. He was telling me not to go to Mamie's too early.

So I caught a subway and went up to the Bronx, killing time walking around, stopping in beer stubes for a couple of drinks, and finally looking at the animals in the Bronx Zoo until the neighborhood movies opened. Then I went into the nearest Loew's and promptly went to sleep. I must have started snoring finally because an usher woke me up. I didn't mind then. It was late afternoon and I felt better. I walked over to the subway and went downtown. I got a shave in a barbershop, bought some pajamas, socks, underwear and a couple of shirts, and then went over to Mamie Bell's.

A mulatto maid opened the door and I said, "Will you tell Miss Bell that Miss Stone's brother is calling?"

She looked suspicious, but went away. Gretchen was there as Miss Stone and I figured my message would tip off Mamie Bell that I was somebody from Pa. A few minutes later, the maid came back and led me up a flight of stairs to a colonial sitting room that should have been transplanted intact to the American Wing of the Metropolitan Museum. The maid was deferential now. Apparently Mamie Bell had taken her cue.

She came in a few moments later. She was a tall woman; a regal woman, and her portrait among your ancestors would have been all the proof you needed of aristocracy. She'd have made a society dowager green with envy.

"I'm Tiberius Bixby," I said. "I hoped my father let you know I was coming."

"When he telephoned about Miss ... er ... Stone, he said you might be able to visit me."

"We're in a jam," I said. "A bad jam. It's swell of you ..."

"You needn't try to explain," she said. "If I don't know the details, then no one can learn them from me. I'm glad you could come."

She sat looking at me a moment with deep, dark eyes, and I wondered if the gentle wave in her mass of white, impeccably coiffed hair was natural. I guessed it wasn't, though. It occurred to me she must have been a beautiful woman, as beautiful as now she was striking. I was wondering why she was so ready to go to bat for Pa when she smiled.

"You do look like your father," she said. "How is he?"

"Oh, Pa's fine. He'll be up here to see me if ... well, if things break right."

"It's been a long time since I saw Zeb," she said. She was half-smiling, but not at me. It was something she was thinking, something she was remembering, that made that fragment of a smile. It made me feel loutishly young. Then she looked at me and rose.

"I'm afraid the old lady will be showing her medals in another moment," she said. "Come, I'll show you to your room. It is on this floor, at the rear, and Miss Stone's is next to it. You will be perfectly safe here, I'm sure. This floor is not used except for my living quarter at the front, and no one else except Annette knows you are here."

We were walking down the hall then. I guessed Annette was the maid. This tall woman walking beside me had me flabbergasted: this gracious lady who was the notorious, the legendary Mamie Bell. She showed me into an immaculate bedroom and then she said, "I hope you'll be comfortable. Just let Annette know if there is anything you need." She paused an instant at the door and studied me a moment with kindly eyes. She didn't look her sixty years or so. There wasn't a wrinkle in her face, nor any mark at all except a few faint lines at the eyes set wide apart and at the nostrils of the finely, firmly chiseled nose.

"You do look like your father," she said again, and gently she closed the door and went away.

I sat wondering, trying to fit the tales I'd heard of Mamie Bell with the woman who had left my room, and for some crazy reason I couldn't get out of my head the picture of the beautiful Empress Carlotta, remembering, in a moment's sanity, Maximilian when he was young and Mexico was only a name on the map.

I tried to snap out of it before I got the sentimental willies. I put on a clean shirt and then I went down the hall to the next room and tapped on the door. Gretchen opened it. I wanted to kiss her, but I said, "It looks like we're going to be neighbors for a while."

"Miss Bell told me you were here," she said. Her voice was strained and when we sat down, the fingers of her hands twined tightly together in her lap. She said, "What's happened? They don't know it was you, do they?"

"I don't think so," I said. I told her about telephoning Pa, but I didn't mention Paula Wannerman. I didn't want to talk about all that. I wanted just to look at her. I tried to think of something that might make her laugh, something that might drive that stricken, harried look out of her eyes, but I couldn't.

"I saw the papers," she said. "Miss Bell brought them. She pretended she didn't recognize my picture. Oh, Tie, she's a darling."

"She's pretty swell, all right. I've heard all the tales about Mamie Bell being a grande dame, but she's not what I figured."

"I know I sound foolish, but ... Oh, I felt so lost and afraid, and then she sat with me a long time, and ... and I didn't feel lost then. I don't know how she did it, but there's something ..."

"Sure," I said. "I know."

Then we sat there a long time, not saying anything, just looking at each other. I had a cigarette in my hand, but I forgot to light it. I don't know how long it was when I got up.

"What about us?" I said.

She looked at me miserably. "I don't know," she said.

"Why did you go into the lavatory when you saw Carr lying there."

"I thought maybe I could help, but ... but he was too far gone, and then ... I lost my head, I guess."

I walked over to the window and stood there looking down into an airshaft, trying to think, but it was all too jumbled in my mind. The way I felt about Gretchen and the suspicion and the murders and Paula Wannerman and Mamie Bell and Pa and ...

Gretchen spoke my name. I turned, and she was standing, looking at me.

"You'd better go," she said. "I ... I want to be alone and try to think."

"Okay," I said. I crushed my cigarette in an ash tray. I said, "You're only hurting yourself by holding out, honey. Why don't you trust Pa and me?"

"I do, Tie, but ... it's too awful ... I can't tell you ... please try to understand and ... Oh, you've been sweet.

I feel like a dog for getting you into this, but ... I can't talk about it now ... I've got to be alone."

She stood with her hands tightly clenched against her sides. She was trying to keep hold of herself. She was looking at me. Her mouth trembled a little.

That was when I kissed her.

Chapter Twelve

The next day, about three o'clock in the afternoon, the maid came to Gretchen's room while we were playing rummy and said I was wanted on the telephone. It was Pa. I was as jumpy as a guy sitting on an ant hill in his B.V.D.'s, but Pa sounded like a man with nothing more pressing on his mind than last Thursday's weather.

"I'm proud of the way you picked up your cue," he said. "I don't think your friend Conner suspected it was you."

"He didn't waste any time getting to town, did he?"

"I regret to say that he's not the sort to waste time or anything else. He is, unfortunately, a very shrewd young man. He wanted to know what Paula Wannerman had told me, so I gave him a complete fill-in.

By way of a climax to my report, I said, "The Wannermans lived in California in 1935."

My climax fell flat. His voice betrayed no more surprise than if I'd told him fire was hot. All he said was, "That wasn't essential to the pattern, of course, but it was a natural supposition. They lived in San Francisco, I presume?"

"Yeah," I said. "Listen, Pa, what's all this about California and 1935 got to do with these murders?"

He ignored my question. "You might tell Miss Jones ... but never mind, I'll wait until the trap is sprung."

He hung up, leaving me spluttering questions. And the newspapers during the days that followed didn't give me any of the answers. It was cold comfort to notice that the Long Island murders had been pushed on an inside page by a slug nutty trombone player who murdered a chorus girl and her two sisters because he couldn't decide which one he loved the best. It didn't help to observe that that was just like a trombone player. For even if the papers had no news, I knew that Rafe Conner and probably the New York cops, too, weren't forgetting those murdered men or Gretchen and me.

We saw Mamie Bell only once. She brought some books and nightgowns and other stuff for Gretchen while we were playing rummy for a thousand bucks a game on the cuff. I was thirty-nine thousand dollars in the hole when she came in and talked for a little while. She didn't mention Pa, so I didn't. When she was gone, Gretchen asked, "Why didn't you talk to her about your father?"

"She didn't ask me about him."

Gretchen frowned impatiently. "Oh, use your head, Tie."

"I'm using it every minute, honey. I'm thinking of all the things we're going to do when this blows over."

"Be serious, Tie. Couldn't you see she was dying to hear everything you could tell her about your dad?"

"I was too busy thinking about us. You know, I've decided you're going to wear a red calot at our wedding."

She put down her cards. "Let's not go through that again," she said.

"And I told you not to be crazy. How many times do

I have to tell you this will all blow over?"

She shook her head. "It won't blow over for me, Tie. I'm in it too deep."

"Then for God's sake tell me everything you know! We can work this out together. We can beat it to some other town, if we have to. Lord, honey, don't you see I love you? Don't you know that whatever the jam is, I'm on your side to the finish?"

She didn't answer for a little while. She sat on the bed looking down at the cards. Then she looked up. Her voice sounded dry, from far off.

"I'd rather have it like this," she said. "I'd rather have these few days."

"But for the love of Mike ..."

"It's your deal," she said.

I picked up the cards, and as I shuffled them to go on with our rummy, the crazy idea came that Gretchen couldn't ever wear a red hat again. For Paula Wannerman had seen her watching the fire and she'd worn a red hat then.

I didn't hear from Pa for five days. The waiting helplessly without knowing what was going on gave us both the jitters, but Gretchen was better at hiding it than I was. On that fifth evening after I came to Mamie Bell's, I suddenly decided I couldn't take it any longer.

"I'm through with this crazy hide-and-seek," I blurted, flinging down my cards. "I'm going out and find what's happened."

"You can't, Tie."

"Just watch me," I said.

"You'll only mess things up, and they're bad enough already."

"Thank you so much for your flattering compliment."

"What good will it do if you're caught and identified

by the taxi driver?"

"It wouldn't be any worse than just sitting here, not knowing what's happening. This is worse than being nibbled by ducks."

"Your father told you to wait until we heard from him."

"I didn't bargain to stay buried forever. Something's happened to him, or he'd have phoned again."

"I think your father can take care of himself a lot better than you can," she said.

"If I'm so dumb, why don't you …"

"Oh, nobody's reflecting on your masculine honor!"

"I'm sorry if my manner irks your ladyship, but I've stood about all I'm going to."

"Look, Tie. Leave this to your father. He … he's uncanny."

There it was again: the strained tone; the fear in her eyes. I knew what she meant. Something in California in 1935—something that had happened then or somebody who had been there then—was at the bottom of this (or damned near it) and she couldn't understand how Pa had known it. Or how much he knew. Well, neither could I. Hell, I didn't even know what it was. He was treating me like a kid too young to hear the facts of life. That galled me.

"Listen, babe," I said, "if you think that because I was dumb enough to fall for you I'm going to be your fall guy in this mess, you've got another think coming. You haven't played on the up-and-up with me, so don't blame me if I do a little watching out for my own neck for a change." Anger made her eyes glint. She was sitting bolt upright on the bed, looking up at me, and her voice was razor-edged.

"I don't remember asking you to meddle in my affairs," she said. "Your absurd chivalry hasn't helped at all, I assure you."

"It's pretty late in the day to be saying that, isn't it? Why didn't you think of that before we had to go on the run? And incidentally, just what would you have done with dear old tuck-waist Tony if I hadn't happened to be along?"

"I would have managed it without the police, at any rate," she said.

"Maybe I could have, too, if you'd shot square. How did you expect me to help you if you wouldn't let me know what the setup was?"

"It ... Oh, drop it! You can go out and introduce yourself to the first policeman you meet if you want to. I don't care. All I ask you is that you leave me alone and stay out of my affairs."

"Okay, Toots, and a Merry Christmas."

I turned toward the door, but she reached me before I got it. Her hand took my arm. I turned, trying to think of a dirty crack. There wasn't any anger in her eyes now, but the fear was still there.

"You can't go," she said.

"Why don't you make up your mind? A moment ago, it was okay by you wherever I went."

"I'm sorry, Tie, really. It was just nerves."

"What would you women do without nerves? You use 'em to justify everything from a binge to running off with the iceman."

"I won't let you go," she said.

"You needn't worry. If the cops get me, I won't squeal where you are."

"Don't be a fool!"

"That's what I'm through being."

"Let's stop being childish, Tie. I don't want you to risk leaving the house. It's not because I'm afraid you'll tell the police. It's because I'm afraid they'll catch you.

It just happens I love you."

It seemed a long time later when I stopped kissing her. She laughed and her eyes were bright and gay.

"What a lot of time we've wasted," she said.

I wanted to laugh and yell, so I kissed her again, and then I told her I'd call a cab and we'd go down to the Municipal Building and get married and taxi back, and nobody would be any the wiser. But she shook her head.

"We can't, Tie. The clerk would be bound to recognize my name."

I felt let down. Then I grinned. "Gee, honey, what a swell honeymoon we'll have! The minute this damned thing is cleared up, we'll …"

She put her fingers gently on my mouth. We stood there a long moment looking at each other, both of us remembering what lay between us, and I wanted to yell at her that she had to tell me how she was tangled in this mess of murder, but the pleading in her eyes more than the fingers on my mouth kept me silent.

"You're sweet, Tie. I'm so sorry."

"Listen, honey, as soon as …"

"Let's not plan, Tie. Let's … Oh, pretend nothing ever happened before this minute! Let's pretend it'll always be now."

"But we've got to think about it," I said. "We've got to figure a way out for you and … damn it, honey, can't you see I can't help you do that if I don't know what's happened? I don't want to talk about it, either, but don't you see I've got to know where you fit into all this?"

She shook her head gently. She was smiling faintly. She was very close to me.

"We've got now," she said, "and it's so very precious."

I was kissing her then, standing with my back to

the door, when a man spoke behind me.

"I suppose this comes under the heading of add 'sweet uses of adversity?'" he said.

It was Pa. He was standing just inside the door, which he'd closed behind him. He stood there, tall, lanky, stooped, with his eyes sunk so deep under the bushy brows that we couldn't tell what was in them. I started to blurt something, but he waved me aside.

"Go right ahead," he said. "I find it a matter for paternal pride to observe such a marked improvement in a son's taste."

Gretchen took his hat and said, "Won't you sit down, Mr. Bixby?"

A sharp catch in her voice made me look at her as Pa took the most comfortable chair in the room, a chintz-covered rocker by the window. All the gaiety was gone from her eyes. She was afraid. The sight of my father had struck her cold with terror. I felt a helpless rage at him as Gretchen and I sat down on the bed and waited for him to speak. He didn't, though. He just slumped down in the chair with his long legs stuck out in front of him and studied us while, sort of absent-mindedly, he twisted the end of his Lafcadio Hearn moustache. I spoke impatiently.

"All right, Pa, take my word for it that it's us. Let's get on with business."

His left eyebrow went up a fraction. "You don't sound in very filial mood," he said.

Gretchen leaned forward suddenly. "Please don't mind him, Mr. Bixby."

"I never mind anyone, Miss Jones. That is why I've never had indigestion."

"Listen," I said, "will you tell us what's happened? God knows you've taken long enough to get around to see us without talking about your digestion."

"You see, Miss Jones, my son is very young. The mark of callow youth is that it regards digestion with disdain. When a man is intellectually mature, he realizes that a good digestion is the one requisite for a satisfactory life. Mind you, I did not say a happy life. A satisfactory life is not necessarily a happy one, nor *vice versa*. Having experience with both, I assure you that a satisfactory life is much the more satisfactory of the two. I recall … "

"For Pete's sake, Pa, cut it! How much longer do we have to stay here?"

Pa fished his corncob pipe out of his pocket. "I don't know," he said.

"How nice," I snapped. "And while you're finding out, I suppose we can go ahead and make our reservations for the booby hatch. That's all we'll be fit for then."

"You amaze me, Tie. What more could anyone want than young love and privacy? With, of course, a good digestion. And you do have an excellent digestion, I believe?"

"Listen, Pa, I'm fed up. I don't want any of your bum humor. I'm going bugs, see? How the hell do you expect us to sit here, not knowing what's up, not knowing …"

"If you don't sit here, you'll be lucky to get off with twenty years," he said.

"That's my funeral. I'm going to get out of here and find out what's happened."

He didn't move, but his voice was suddenly harsh. His words were like slaps in the face.

"You'll do nothing of the kind," he said. "You will stay here until I tell you to leave. You have a perfect right to endanger your own neck by being an addlepated fool, but you have no right to place others in danger."

"Say, can't you get it through your head that I'm

free, white and twenty-one?"

"You're exhibiting the intelligence of a two-year-old," he said. "Are you such a blithering ass that you can't see it's essential for you to lay low until this is cleared up?"

"That's all very true, but just the same ..."

"You'll do as I say, Tie. We Bixbys have done a number of reprehensible things in our lives, but none of us has ever been such a fool that he was caught by either husbands or the police. And I do not intend to have the family made ridiculous by having you go to prison for being a silly blunderer."

"And suppose I disagree with you?"

"It is not a matter for argument," he said. He sounded downright pontifical. "You should know that my standard of values is rigid, if unorthodox. You know I can tolerate any crime except stupidity. And I believe quite firmly that the greatest sin a family—or an empire—can commit is to become ridiculous. It is invariably fatal. If you question the point. I would suggest that you read ..."

"This isn't any time for a history lecture! What's happened? What've you done?"

"Well," he said, drawing an envelope out of his inside pocket, "you might find these interesting."

He tossed me the envelope, and out of it I took a couple of photographs of a slick-haired young man. He was wearing a stiff collar high enough to choke a giraffe.

"That's your friend Wannerman in his college days," he said. "Thanks to your lead, I found the college yearbook at the library and had his photographs copied. Mean looking devil, isn't he?"

"A fine lot of help these are. Oh, I knew why you were so hot to get a picture of him. You figured—and give me credit for doing it, too—that he might have been running some racket under cover of his science and that racket might have been the cause of his death. Even I was able to figure that with a photo of him we'd stand a lot better chance of finding somebody who'd recognize him as having been in this racket, whatever it was."

"If there was such a racket," Pa put in mildly.

"Whether there was or wasn't, these pictures won't be much help to you. They're twenty years old."

"Still," Pa said, taking back the pictures, "they're interesting. You can learn a lot about what kind of character he had by studying these pictures."

"I'm not interested in a dead man's character. I'm interested in my neck, mine and Gretchen's."

He ignored me. He sat with his lips pursed, closely studying the clearest of the photographs, talking as though to himself without looking up at the silent, staring girl or me.

"When you want to understand a man's enemies, you must first understand the man; what manner of being he was beneath the surface. Now consider this profile. It is an uncurtained window to his soul. The very tilt of the head tells us he was arrogant, cocksure, conceited. More to the point, consider the low forehead, that strange cleft in his chin, the lobeless ears, the unusual way his mouth pinched at the corners, the flare of the nostrils from a pointed nose—surely, such a man must come to a bad end. Surely what we learn of his character from this observation will be valuable in determining who …"

I couldn't take it any longer. I stood up and said, "God damn it, Pa, will you quit the gab? Let's decide what we're going to do."

"I thought we were progressing quite satisfactorily,"

he said. He seemed mildly surprised.

"Why give us a lot of bilge out of Lombroso? All that phiz reading stuff is the bunk, and you know it. It's as discredited as the British Empire's foreign policy."

He smiled gently. "Maybe you're right, Tie. I have been sort of rough on you, but your bumptiousness rather irritated me. Especially when you've been so lacking in perception as not to see how the case was building itself."

"What do you mean, building itself?"

"We aren't out of the woods yet, not by a long shot, and there's danger and death still ahead, but …"

He shrugged, sat silent a moment sucking slowly on his pipe, and then he went on: "Think back over everything, Tie, and you're bound to see what I mean. Damn it, boy, you've got to use your head, and you won't if I tell you all the answers."

"All right, Father Sherlock, just tell me one of the answers, if you've got so many."

The narrowing of his eyes should have warned me. He's a good egg, but he's got a mean streak when he's irked.

"If one answer is all you need, perhaps Miss Jones will supply it."

She sprang up before I could speak. Then she seemed suddenly to wilt. Her voice was entreating, desperate.

"Please," she said. "Please. Don't …"

Pa looked at her steadily a moment. "I'm sorry," he said.

"Oh, I know it's bound to come out. I know I can't hide it forever. But please, not yet."

"It's got to happen sometime," he said.

She nodded dully. I felt as though somebody had clubbed me. I stood up and put my arm around her, but she didn't seem to know I was there. She was staring at the tall, old man sprawled in the chair. Then the words came in a pleading rush.

"Nothing can help. I know that, Mr. Bixby. The thing is done and ... and I can't get away. I won't try. I swear I won't. Only ... Oh, it doesn't have to be now, does it?"

It seemed a long time before Pa answered. Then he said, "No, it doesn't have to be now."

I felt the girl's tense body relax. Suddenly, as though something had collapsed within her, she bent her head into her hands and began to sob. I tried to comfort her, but she turned from me and slumped down on the bed. I whirled on Pa. I wanted to bash him.

"I've had enough! Tell me what this is all about or so help me God ..."

"Oh, shut up," he said wearily.

I started for him, but stopped short. I hadn't seen him move, but his right hand was holding a pistol pointed at me. I gawked at it stupidly.

"That's better," he said. "I'm too old to slug it out with you and I have no intention of being manhandled, not even by my son. If you attempt it, Tie, I'll have to shoot you."

The girl cried out. He spoke to her, but his eyes—and the gun—never wavered from me by so much as a flicker.

"You needn't be alarmed," he said. "I wouldn't kill a son of mine, not even one as birdbrained as Tie. But I assure you, I will break both of his legs if he doesn't sit down and stay quiet."

The girl tried to draw me down on the bed beside her. Pa's voice was chill.

"I repeat, you had better sit down. You may remember I'm rather good with a pistol."

I sat down beside the girl. She was holding tightly to my arm. I stared at my father.

"You deserve a swift kick in the pants," he said. "If you haven't enough understanding to figure this out now, there's no hope for you."

I didn't answer. It was all too jumbled. I felt sick. I wanted to crawl off somewhere and cry. I hadn't felt like that since I was a kid.

"There's no need to sit there like an egg's busted in you," he said. "My Lord, haven't you got eyes and ears?"

Still I didn't say anything. I couldn't. If I'd spoken, I'd have blubbered. I was damned if I'd let him see me do that.

He slipped the pistol into the side pocket of his baggy grey coat. It occurred to me dully that I'd never seen my father in anything except heavy suits that needed pressing.

"Sorry," he said curtly. "I didn't mean to get to rambling like a grazing goat."

He got up and put on his hat. He stood a moment looking down at me, but I didn't lift my eyes. I could have grabbed him then. I could have choked the answers out of him. But I didn't want to anymore. The anger was gone out of me. There was left only the dull thinking over and over, *Gretchen ... nothing can help ... it must come out ... Gretchen did it....* There was only that and a lost feeling inside of me. I was licked.

Pa said, "Sorry, son."

His voice was quiet and he put his hand a moment on my shoulder. I nodded. It didn't seem to matter. Gretchen stood up. She held my head against her body. She was stroking my head.

Pa said, "Damn it, son, why don't you use your brain? Doesn't Schwartz mean anything to you?"

I felt the girl's body stiffen against my cheek. Fear

must have showed in her face, for Pa said, "All right, I won't tell him, then. But you're being a fool, young woman. Why don't you get it over with?"

I heard Pa open the door. He spoke only once more: just four words. They stunned us so he was gone before we could stop him.

"Dirck Wannerman's still alive," he said.

PART TWO

Here the telling of the tale is taken up
by old Zeb Bixby from the time he left
his son and Gretchen Jones at Mamie Bell's.

Chapter Thirteen

As I closed the door, I knew I had solved the mystery of the murders in silk.

I am a conceited old man and so it was strange that I felt no elation at the realization that I had formed a perfect pattern without any clues except the jumble of information my son has duly recorded in this book and which, if you've read this far, you know as well as I do.

It occurred to me as I walked wearily along the hall that my pattern did lack one requisite of perfection. I had yet to prove it. I knew, though, that only two things could block me from this proof—the chance that Paula Wannerman would betray me and the chance that I might be the third man murdered.

Then I saw Mamie Bell. I had not seen her when I came to the house. She had sent the maid to take me to Gretchen's room with the word that she would see me later. Now she was waiting for me at the head of the stairs, wearing a black evening dress, and her eyes were bright even in the dimness of the hall.

She put out her hand. The skin was still soft to touch after all these years. We didn't speak for a moment. We just stood there looking at each other: an old man in a shabby suit, a tired old man, and an old woman who didn't look old. We had not seen each other in forty years.

"I knew you would come someday," she said.

She was smiling now. I wondered how I had forgotten her smile.

"I knew Tess would write you what had become of me," she said. "Tess always hated me so much I knew I could depend on her."

She laughed softly, and her laughter still had ripples in it.

"That's why I've always kept my telephone number listed," she said. "I knew some day you would call me."

I tried to say something, tried to thank her, but words are not easy when you are seventy, when you have tortured your son, when you wonder if, after all, you have learned anything from living.

"I'm glad he's here," she said. "He looks like you did, Zeb. It was almost like seeing you."

There didn't seem to be anything I could say. Mamie Bell was saying something, but I was trying to remember and I didn't hear her. She stopped. She was looking at me steadily, not saying anything, and then she put her hand a moment on my arm. I knew it was time to go.

"It's been a long time," I said. It was strange, but there didn't seem to be anything else to say. There was a moment of uneasy silence between us, and then I said, because I had to say something, "Forty years, that's a long time."

She smiled faintly. "And besides," she said, "the wench is dead."

So I went on down the stairs slowly, feeling tired and uncertain, which was unusual for me, since I long ago realized that only sureness of oneself—conceit, if you will—can protect a man against the disastrous realization of his own supreme unimportance.

I went out the door and into the dark street, and behind me I knew Mamie Bell was still looking down the empty stair.

It occurred to me that for a man who has lived seventy years, I was an awful fool. No blithering young nincompoop—not even an Efficiency Expert—could have made a more abysmal mess of things than I had done with Tie and Gretchen Jones in the girl's room. I had let him irritate me so that I badgered him and then I couldn't tell him what I knew. With him loving the girl as he did, I couldn't take the chance that he wouldn't do something crazy in an attempt to save her. Then, unable to resist the temptation to show off, I'd told him that Wannerman wasn't dead.

"It's bad enough to be seventy, without acting your age," I said aloud, and a bottle-bottomed woman with her arms full of bundles stopped to stare at me.

I clumped on down the street to a bar, reflecting that the only excuse I could offer for myself was that I'd been sober at Mamie Bell's. When a man reaches my age, he cannot expect to be sober with impunity. That is, he can't unless he has frittered away his life on sobriety.

I felt better after a drink. I reflected that whiskey is the sovereign remedy for all ills of the spirit, though naturally not adequately appreciated among tribes so barbarous that they still consider cocktails as fit for human consumption.

I glanced at the clock on the wall. It was after eight: time to check with Paula Wannerman. I went into the telephone booth at the end of the bar and called Tie's apartment. Paula answered the phone.

"We drew another blank," she said. "I'm beginning to think she'll never show up."

"She's bound to go there sooner or later," I said. "All we've got to do is to keep on trying."

"It's getting me down. It's worse because I have to go along in the dark, not knowing what your plan is. I tell you, Mr. Bixby, I'm getting the heebies."

"That was our deal," I reminded her.

"Oh, I'm not forgetting, but the sledding's kind of tough."

I told her I'd be home right away and then I hung up and went back to the bar for another Irish. I felt sorry for Paula, but there wasn't anything I could do for her. I needed her help, but I couldn't trust her; couldn't tell her what I knew. For one thing, I didn't know how much she knew or how much more she suspected. And above all, I couldn't take a chance on what her reaction might be if I laid all my cards on the table.

I didn't pretend to myself that I'd been fair with Paula Wannerman. I got her to come to the flat by telephoning and pretending that Tie wanted to see her. She was blazing mad at me for the trick, but I told her I had to do it because Tie was in danger.

"They're trying to get him for the murder of your father and that man on the train," I said. "He's innocent and I've got to prove it. Once those cops get their hands on him, they'll have him framed and in the electric chair before he knows what's happening. That's why I called you. That's why I want your help."

She had sat dead-white while I was talking, all the anger drained out of her, and then she said she would help me. Her mother was going back to her family's home in Seattle, and the girl said she'd come and stay with me at Tie's flat.

I lied to her; told her I didn't know what the setup really was; that I was groping in the dark. I don't think she believed me, but she didn't say so.

"I don't know whether Tie's guilty or not," she said. "I don't care. I guess you think I'm a fool?"

"No," I said, "I merely think you love him."

"I do," she said quietly.

So we had a drink to our alliance, and next morning Paula Wannerman began covering Charmaine's beauty parlor from a bar across the street. A ten-spot to the owner made it all right for her to sit with a book at a table at the front of the place where she could keep watch through the plate glass window. He thought she was a private detective getting divorce evidence, and that was perfectly all right with him since he was promised another ten dollars on the first of each week she used the bar.

"There's a chance you'll miss her, and we're wrecked if you do," I told her. "We've got to get Stella Vardis."

She was suspicious, but then she said, "I'll play it your way, Mr. Bixby. I guess I've got to. But I don't understand."

She wanted to see Tie, of course, but I told her he was in hiding; that I wouldn't risk telling even her where he was. She had to be content with that during the days she watched from the bar for Stella Vardis to come to Charmaine's beauty salon. I spent most of the time with her. I guess the saloon keeper thought I was the December husband checking up on my April wife. I didn't tell him any different. And I had better sense than to mention Gretchen Jones to Paula.

This all ran through my head as I stood drinking my third Irish and water. I decided to have one more and then go down to Jane Street and lie a little to Paula; tell her that Tie had talked about her. It would make her feel better, but that wasn't my reason. I had an idea that the lie would keep her in line, and I had to have her help. If I didn't, I might not recognize Stella Vardis even from the photographs I'd studied at the *World-Telegram* morgue. And even if I would have known her, my eyes weren't good enough to trust them to recognize anybody at that distance.

I nodded to the bartender. "The same," I said, and he pushed the bottle toward me for my stirrup cup. I had just lifted the bottle to pour my drink when somebody beside me spoke.

"Make it two," he said.

It was Rafe Conner. His mouth was smiling in quiet triumph, but his eyes were flinty. I kept a deadpan and passed him the bottle. He was chewing gum, of course.

"I thought I'd lost you in Times Square," I said casually.

"You did. That's what you were supposed to do. I figured if you were busy losing me, you wouldn't notice Joe. He tailed you all the way up here and I made myself comfortable until he phoned me where you were."

"Smart work," I said. "Too bad you had all your trouble for nothing. If I'd known, I'd have tried to go somewhere interesting."

"You did all right, Mr. Bixby. You did just what I wanted you to, and Joe's got the house covered right now."

"Maybe I'm getting senile, Conner, but I confess I can't see why you're in such a dither about the house. I just went by to see an old friend."

"Sure, Mamie Bell. I checked up on that while you were inside."

"Look here," I said, making a bluff of it. "I don't know what you're up to, but you seem well on the way to making a sap of yourself. Why the sudden interest in retired madames?"

"Because Tie and Gretchen Jones are inside," he said.

I feigned surprise. "I wish you'd told me before. I'd have stopped to see them. I've been wondering where Tie went myself."

He shook his head slowly, and I went on impatiently. "You're being crazier than I thought," I said. "Do you think I'd be fool enough to go where my son is, even if I knew, when I realized very well that I was being tailed?"

"It won't go, Mr. Bixby." He took a sip of his drink and then nodded to one of the booths that lined the wall opposite the bar. He said, "Let's sit down over here where we can talk a little more privately."

I followed him to the booth and we sat down facing each other across the table. He lit a cigarette and took a couple of slow drags before he spoke. I waited with the best poker face I could manage.

"I don't blame you for trying to protect them," he said. "I'd have done the same thing in your place. But you can't help 'em now, Mr. Bixby. It's all over but the shouting."

I didn't answer. I was trying to figure some out now that I'd botched everything; now that Conner had tricked me into trapping my son and the girl. And trapping Mamie Bell, too, for she was bound to be carried down in the crash because she'd hid them. It was one thing for me to know Tie was innocent; that he had nothing to do with the murders, but it was another thing to prove it. And if Rafe Conners got his hands on them, I could see what a fat chance I'd have of ever cracking the case. I'd have the same chance that a gob of butter has in a sizzling skillet. They'd laugh at me if I tried to convince them.

Something of what I was thinking must have showed in my face, for Conner's tone was kindly as, turning his glass slowly in his thick fingers, he went on.

"Joe's covering the house, and they can't get away," he said. "Once we get to work on 'em, they'll crack. I don't know just how much Tie knows—nothing, I hope—but that girl's got the answer to these murders."

I nodded wearily. "To one of them, anyway," I said.

He studied me a moment and then he said, "I know where that Gurkha knife came from. I remembered where I'd seen it before."

"From the description I read, I'd say there were a great many knives like it."

"Not in this case. Elephant heads aren't usual on the hilts. And Tie's the only person I ever saw playing with a Gurkha knife like that. We were kids and …"

"All right, so what? You didn't stop me to talk about Gurkha knives and boyhood memories."

"No, sir, I didn't." He pressed his lips together and frowned, munching his gum as he framed his sentences.

I waited. I felt strangely detached. I knew that only two things were important now. No harm or scandal must come to any of my children. And whatever she had done, I had to save Gretchen Jones, if I could, because my son loved her.

"I'll lay my cards on the table," Conner said. "Before I called the New York cops to make the pinch, I wanted to talk to you. I don't want to have to be any tougher than I have to, Mr. Bixby. If you help me, if you tell me what you know—and I figure you know plenty, or suspect it—well, I'll do what I can for Tie."

I knew it was the old police stall, but I played along. I asked him what the other detectives said about it.

"They don't know from nothing," he said. "I haven't

told anybody but Joe and I'm not telling anybody until I lay this case right in their laps, signed, sealed and delivered. That dope of a chief has been riding my neck plenty long, and I'm going to have all the credit for breaking this."

That settled it. He could deliver on a bargain with me, if he would. If he wouldn't ...

"Well, Mr. Bixby, what about it?"

"What do you want to know?"

"All that you know," he said. "I'll tell you frankly, I haven't got all the pieces of this puzzle in the right places. I'll admit that because you know it, anyhow. But once Tie and the Jones girl talk—and don't ever think they won't spill their guts—then I'll know just what happened."

"You're chasing yourself down a blind alley," I said. "They can talk till the Judgment Day, and you'll still be as far from breaking this case as I am from being Queen of the May."

"I don't bluff worth a damn, Mr. Bixby. I want you to help me because that'll make things easier, but I can still crack it wide open if you don't."

"You're trying the bluff, Conner. I've got this case in the bag, and that's where it stays unless you play my way."

"Suppose I run you in, too? How'd you like that?"

"You wouldn't be that stupid," I said, taking out my pipe, filling it carefully, lighting it before I went on. He watched me closely.

"Let's hear your proposition," he said.

"I'll make a deal with you," I said. "If you get Tie and the Jones girl in the clear—clear of everything, I mean, the fight at her apartment and the rest—then I'll crack the case for you."

"I'm afraid you'll have to do your cracking first. I've

got to be sure you can deliver."

I hesitated. If I told him what I'd figured out, there was nothing to prevent him collaring Tie and Gretchen, anyhow. I had to take the gamble, though. He was bound to arrest them if I didn't.

So I told Rafe Conner what I'd figured out, holding back nothing. I saw the incredulous disbelief fade from his eyes, replaced by astounded realization, as I laid each brick of logic in its proper place until the structure of my case was complete—except for the clinching proof.

"So don't you see Tie and the girl don't matter right now?" I ended. "It's Stella Vardis you've got to get."

"If I can do that, finding a needle dropped into Long Island Sound will be a cinch."

"You don't have to worry about the other one," I said. "I'll hear the minute that one tries to run out."

"The way you've told it is so damned pat it worries me," he said. "You've clean overlooked Nicky Pet and his gangsters."

"I didn't overlook them; I eliminated them. You see, Conner, a police department can afford to go at a case in a logical, routine way, checking everything to its source before they make up their minds. But one man trying to solve a mystery like this can't do that. He hasn't got the facilities. He has to take a chance on ... well, a theory."

"Well," he said, "I don't know whether you've got the right one, but damned if it doesn't seem right."

"Then it's a deal?"

"If I was sure you were right about Stella Vardis and could get it out of her ..."

"I know I can," I said. "The chances are about a million to one she hasn't skipped town. We're up against a smart brain, and a smart brain will know that New York is the safest place in the world to hide. Anyhow, there's not the faintest reason for anybody to suspect that we're even suspicious of her."

"That sounds all right," he said.

"Then if she hasn't left New York, we're bound to get her. It's just a question of waiting a few days until she shows up at Charmaine's."

"The beauty parlor you mentioned?"

"That's it," I said. "Miss Wannerman and I are keeping it covered, and when Stella Vardis shows up, I'll tail her to wherever she goes, find her hideout, and then ..."

I snapped my fingers. "The rest of it's as easy as that," I said.

"I wish I was as sure as you are that she'll go to this Charmaine's," he said. "I don't see any reason to suspect she'd be fool enough to walk into your trap."

"She'll come. She hasn't the faintest idea that everything isn't going like clockwork. So why should she stay away?"

"Why should she go?" he retorted. "Why shouldn't she go to any other beauty shop in town, if she's got to go to one?"

"Don't be dense, man! Can't you remember what Paula Wannerman told Tie about Vardis?"

"I still don't see what's to make her so obliging that she'll toddle right into your trap. She doesn't sound that considerate to me."

"Look here," I said. "She's a beautiful woman, beauty's her main stock in trade. Now she's got dyed blonde hair that has to be touched up every week or ten days. And she says the only person she ever found who did her hair right was Charmaine."

"Which doesn't mean ..."

My impatience blazed up. "Don't you see that she's

bound to come out of her hole to have her hair fixed? She thinks there's nothing in the world to connect her with the murders. So she'll start telling herself it'll be perfectly safe to go to Charmaine's, have her hair fixed and then drop out of sight again."

"Hold on a minute," he interrupted. "What's to keep her from having them send somebody to do her hair? Then you and the Wannerman girl wouldn't know about it."

"The chances are that Charmaine doesn't go out on jobs herself, and don't forget it's Charmaine, and not her assistants, who's the world's one perfect hair dyer in Vardis' eyes. Even if Charmaine would go out on the job, Vardis is bound to be too smart to have her come to the hideout. And if Vardis went to a hotel and had Charmaine come there, she's bound to know that would cause talk, which is the one thing she doesn't want. So I think we can be pretty sure that Vardis will come to the shop."

"I wish I was as sure as you are," he said, frowning doubtfully.

"She's bound to do it. Since she doesn't know we're on to her, the temptation to have her hair touched up will be too strong to resist when she sees the black beginning to show at the roots. It's the most rudimentary feminine psychology."

He sat preoccupied, frowning as he turned over in his mind all I had told him. Finally, he crushed out the stub of his cigarette and spoke brusquely.

"I'll do it," he said. "I'll string along with you a few days. I won't touch Tie and the girl if they stay put. But Joe and I'll keep the house covered twenty-four hours a day, and if they make a break for it, we'll have to grab 'em."

"Fair enough," I said. "And after we've broken the

case?"

He hesitated a long moment before he answered. "I'm pretty sure I can put in a fix for Tie, if he isn't involved in the murders. They'll be sore, but I don't think there's much danger they won't square it, if there isn't any kick. And I don't guess that rat Tie bashed up will do much complaining."

"I rather think not," I said.

"I can't promise about the girl, though. I'll try, sure, but she's in one hell of a spot."

I had to be content with that and play the hand as it was dealt.

"I'll cover the house nights and let Joe take it days," he went on. "I'll spend all day at a hotel, the nearest one to the beauty shop. I'll let you know which one, and you call me the minute the Vardis dame shows up. I'll get right over and be on her tail when she leaves. That's the only way I can make the deal. I can't take a chance …"

"I understand," I said.

"I can't string along forever, Mr. Bixby. I'm sorry, but if we don't show results in a few days, I'll have to call it a bad gamble. I'll have to run in Tie and the girl and take my chances on what I get out of them. I'll still do my best for Tie, though, if he'll open up."

"I see your position," I said. "All I ask is that you give me a day's warning before you tip the New York police to pick them up."

He looked at me with sudden suspicion. "I want time to make arrangements for bailing him. I don't want Tie to have to stay in the Tombs. It's not asking a lot, since they can't get away."

"I know they can't," he said. "I've already checked that there's no way out the back of that house."

"Do I get my day?"

"Maybe I'm being a soft sap, but okay," he said. "I'll give you twelve hours notice before I call the locals to make the collar. But I warn you, Mr. Bixby, if you try anything funny ..."

"Just what do you think I could do?"

He grinned, unwrapping a fresh stick of gum. "Nothing," he said, "absolutely nothing."

I got up to leave and we shook hands. He said he'd telephone me to let me know his hotel the first thing in the morning. He seemed embarrassed then, as big men usually are by their own decency.

"I hope it works," he said. "If anybody had ever told me I'd make a crazy deal like this ..."

"It will work," I said. "It's got to."

I left him then and got a taxi at the corner. When I got home, Paula Wannerman was sitting by the empty fireplace, smoking nervously.

"I thought you'd never get here," she said. "I thought something had happened."

"Something did. Rafe Conner trailed me to Tie's hideout."

She went white. I thought for a moment she was going to keel over. She spoke as though it was hard to get out the words.

"Did he ... was Tie arrested?"

"Not yet," I said. I told her what had passed between the detective and me, omitting only one thing. I did not mention Gretchen Jones.

She sat staring at me as I talked, and she ran her hand nervously back through the blonde hair as I finished. Her voice shook.

"She's got to come! She's got to!"

"She will," I said.

She crushed out her cigarette. Then immediately she lit another one, smoking it with quick puffs. She realized what she'd done and gave a quick, hard laugh.

"You must think I'm crazy," she said. "Maybe I am. I can't stand thinking what may happen to Tie."

I got up and went to the cabinet in the corner. "You need a drink," I said. "I think we both do."

"I need a flock of drinks," she said, but when I brought her a highball, she only sipped it and put it down on the coffee table and forgot about it.

"There's something I've got to know," she blurted. "I know you don't trust me, and I don't blame you for not telling me what you think of all this, but you've got to tell me this one thing."

I looked at her from the chair where I slouched with my legs stretched out. I didn't want to talk. I was seventy years old and I was tired.

"You've got to tell me the truth," she said. "Is Tie with that girl?"

"I'm afraid that's hardly specific, but as nobody happens to be with him, I can tell you the answer is 'No.'"

"You aren't lying to me, are you? You aren't just saying that?"

"My dear young woman, I haven't the faintest idea what you're driving at."

"That Jones girl, the one in the papers. She's disappeared, and ... well, there was a man with her and ..."

"I remember her now," I said, "but I don't see what she's got to do with Tie!"

"The description of the man was ... well, it could have been Tie."

I forced myself to laugh, leaning my head on the back of the chair. She flushed angrily.

"It could have been him," she said.

"It could have been a million or so other men in New

York, too. Haven't we got enough to worry about without looking for goblins under the bed?"

"I suppose so," she said.

She sat smoking in silence. She looked so miserable that I made up a lie that Tie had talked a lot about her, complimentary stuff and all that. I knew I was probably storing up a harder jolt for her when she found out about Gretchen, but I did it, anyhow. She didn't say anything as I went on, spinning out the tale, and she sat quietly smoking for a few minutes after I was done. Then she got up and said she was going to bed. She paused at the door and turned to look at me. She was smiling slightly.

"That was kind of you," she said. "It was nice to hear, even if it wasn't true."

Chapter Fourteen

At eleven o'clock the next morning, I was awakened by the telephone. It was Paula. She'd gone to cover the beauty shop without waking me. Her voice was shaking.

"She's here! I just saw her go into Charmaine's!"

I'd had my plan of action arranged from the day I set the trap for Stella Vardis, but I muffed the start of it. I was in such a flurry of haste after Paula phoned that I didn't take time to shave and clomped off down the stairs without taking the bundle that was an essential part of my plan. I didn't realize I'd forgotten it until I was in a taxi rolling north on Eighth Avenue and by that time it occurred to me that my hurry was silly. I had neglected to find out how long it took a synthetic blonde to get her hair touched up, but I felt sure it would take considerably longer than a shave and haircut. So I told the driver to stop at the first haberdashery he saw and wait for me.

I bought a blue shirt, three handkerchiefs and a red necktie. I bustled back to the cab with my bundle and, as he threaded his way through the morning traffic, I enlisted the driver as an ally by promising him a five-dollar tip if I got what I wanted.

"A fin's a lot of dough, mister, but it ain't enough to get in a jam about."

"There won't be any," I said. "I'm after a woman who jumped her lease, and all I want is to find out where she lives now."

"Okay, but the first sign of trouble, I check out."

"Both of us do," I said. "This woman is at a beauty shop where we're going. There's no cab stand in that block, so you can pull up to the curb a couple of doors away. Keep your flag down and let 'er tick so nobody can hire you. I'll be across the street, and when I give you the high sign, you throw your flag up and roll up, so if she takes a cab, she'll take you."

"Suppose she don't take me?"

"If she walks over to get a subway, I'll follow her on foot, and the young lady who'll be with me will pay you off. If she has a car or a cab come to pick her up, I'll follow her in your cab."

"What'll I do if she takes me?" he said.

"I'll follow you in another cab. Go slow until you're sure I'm following and be sure you don't lose us. After you let her out, go on to the next corner, and I'll follow you there and pay you off."

He was studying me suspiciously in his rear-view mirror, and so I said, "I'll pay you for this ride first, if you want it."

He hesitated and then said, "No need of that. You don't look like no chiseler."

I leaned back in the seat. There was always the chance that something would come up, of course, but I couldn't think of any precaution I could have taken that I hadn't arranged to take. There was one danger I couldn't guard against, of course: the danger that Paula Wannerman was playing a double-crossing game. There was nothing to show she was, but nothing to show she wasn't, either. Her sudden love for Tie was hard to believe, but such things do happen, though rarely. I had to gamble she was playing straight with me because I needed her, and the rest of that gamble was that I'd be able to block her if she did try a false play. I hadn't forgotten to slip my gun in my pocket, and that was lucky. I was likely to need it.

My driver—his name was Wilmer Katz—drew up two doors from the beauty shop, which had a cream-colored facade, ruffled drapes covering the windows and *Charmaine* in Neon script above the door.

"I'll stand across the street," I said. "When our woman comes out of the beauty shop, I'll take off my hat, and you go for her. If she walks, my ... er ... secretary will, come from that bar and pay you."

Mr. Katz craned his neck and saw Paula looking at us from the wide glass front of the bar. That seemed to satisfy.

"Okay," said Mr. Katz.

I hurried to the bar. Paula smiled when she saw me, but her hand shook as she lifted her drink.

"You made good time," she said.

I laid my bundle down on the table. She looked at it questioningly, but I didn't explain. I told her I'd be right back and walked down to the corner and flagged a cab.

"A woman will come out of that beauty shop and take that cab across the street," I said. "I want to follow her to wherever she's going. Here's a dollar for your trouble if she doesn't take the cab, and there'll be another dollar at the end of the trip if she does and you don't lose her."

He looked at me suspiciously, but said, "I gotcha. She won't get away from me if we get half a break on the lights."

I went back to the bar. I glanced at my watch. It had been almost an hour since Paula had phoned me. Her jitters were getting worse, but she was trying to hide them. The suspicion flashed through my head that maybe she was so nervous because she was about to cross me up, but I shrugged that off. It was too late to change signals now.

"I'll wait outside," I said. "The instant you see her coming out, knock on the window. Then turn your back. There's just a chance she might recognize you if she looks over here."

She nodded, and I went out to the sidewalk, my bundle under my arm. I lit my pipe and stood with my back to the street as though I was reading the bar's menu pasted in the window. The proprietor looked at me closely, but he earned his ten dollars by keeping out of the way.

It seemed like hours passed, but when I glanced at my watch, I saw I'd been standing there only forty minutes. I was feeling tired, though. The excitement, I guessed. I went back into the bar.

"She's taking an awful long time," I said. "How long does a touchup take?"

"About an hour," Paula said. "I suppose she's having a manicure, too."

I returned to my study of the menu from the sidewalk. I should have called Rafe Conner, I suppose, but I didn't want him in on it. I'd have a lot more to bargain with for Tie and the girl if I knew where Stella Vardis was and he didn't.

Paula knocked sharply on the window. I took off my hat. I turned casually and saw Mr. Katz throw his flag up as though he'd just let out a fare. On the curb in front of Charmaine's was a tall, bored-looking blonde dressed in a blue and green print. She seemed undecided about something, and then she nodded imperiously to the cabbie. He rolled up to her, and she got in. His engine stopped and he had to start it again. By the time they reached the corner, my bundle and I were only ten or fifteen feet behind in the second cab.

"Be careful you don't get too close," I told the driver. "I don't want her to see me."

"I gotcha."

I saw the woman lean forward and say something to her driver. He swung north, then east, and headed into Central Park. Her wish to ride through the park simplified our task. The park was behind us and we were far north of Harlem when my driver said, "Looks like they're going to the Bronx."

But the woman's cab bore west, then north, then west again along 181st Street. The great span of George Washington Bridge was just below us, and I thought they might be circling to come at it from uptown, but when they were a block from the Hudson River, the cab turned north again.

We were rolling along a narrow street of modern apartment houses. The cab ahead swung to the curb. A hallman in uniform was standing in the doorway and he went forward to open the taxi door for her. She didn't glance at us as we went by.

"What street's this?" I asked.

"Search me. I'm from Brooklyn myself."

The street curved a short distance below the

apartment house, and I told the driver to stop. I looked back. Stella Vardis was entering the house. The hallman followed her in. I watched to see whether anybody else went in. The other cab pulled up behind mine, and my friend, Mr. Wilmer Katz, grinned at me.

"Well, that's doing it, ain't it, mister."

"Perfectly," I said. "Just a second while I pay off my driver."

I gave him his fare and the dollar, and he pulled away, glancing over his shoulder as though suspecting the beaming Mr. Katz and me of being up to no good. Mr. Katz said we were on Northern Avenue and he handed me a slip of paper with a number written on it.

"That's her address in case you didn't get the number."

"Thanks," I said. "Did she say anything coming up?"

"Not a crack except she told me to go through the park."

"Did the flunkey mention her name, call her anything."

"He just said, 'Good afternoon.' He knows her, though, because she called him 'Fred.'"

I gave him the fare I'd owed him and the five dollars I'd promised for a tip. Mr. Katz beamed, but seemed severely disappointed when I told him I didn't want him to wait. I was tempted to try to bribe him to play my role for me, or at least rent me his cap and badge, but I realized I couldn't take the risk. So I watched him drive away reluctantly and then walked back to the apartment house. If the hallman came out, I'd have to change my stall, but he didn't. I'd kept watch while I paid off the drivers, and nobody had entered the house after Stella Vardis. I took a deep breath and walked in with my bundle.

The hallman was sitting in a chair in the lobby. I went over to him and said, "A lady just came in here …"

He didn't volunteer her name, so I went on, "She dropped this bundle when she got out of a cab. I happened to see her from down the street."

"I'll give it to her," he said. He got up and put out his hand, but I kept the package.

"I want to give it to her myself," I said.

He looked at me disapprovingly. "What's the idea?" he demanded.

"Maybe she'll give me something," I said. I was glad then I hadn't shaved. The stubble made me look seedier. "I'm pretty much up against it and any little thing'll help. You just tell me what apartment she's in and I'll take it up."

"We don't allow that," he snapped. "I'll phone up to her."

"She'll just say bring it up and won't give me nothing."

"That ain't my funeral, grandpa."

"I tell you what, son. You let me go up and I'll split with you anything I get."

"Fat chance," he said, but he didn't lift the house phone.

"Come along with me, then, and you can see what she gives me."

"Okay, grandpa, but don't try no funny business."

He led the way to the automatic elevator and pushed the button for the seventh floor.

"She looked like money to me," I said. "She ought to be good for a buck, don't you think so?"

"You're lucky to get 'thank you' out of the Duchess," he said.

"Duchess? She's a real duchess?"

He smirked scornfully. "Naw, she's just a tomato

that's got her nose in the air. We call her the Duchess 'cause she's so snotty. She's been here six months now, off and on, and she hasn't give a one of us the right time."

"Maybe she's a high class floozie," I said.

"Naw, she's got a husband. He's a travelling man. She used to go on his trips with him sometimes, but now she says she's tired of travelling."

We were at our floor and he led the way to an apartment door lettered "7-A." A card was stuck in the pushbell slot:

David P. Lewis

My sour-faced companion rang the bell. There was a long wait and then the door was opened an inch on the safety chain and a woman spoke.

"What is it?"

"It's Fred, Mrs. Lewis. There's a man here says he found a bundle you dropped. He wouldn't give it to me, so I brought him up."

There was a long pause. Then I heard the chain rattle and the door opened. Stella Vardis looked at me suspiciously. A radio was playing inside the apartment.

"I didn't drop a bundle," she said. 'What makes you think it's mine?"

"I'm sorry if I made a mistake, lady, but I saw you get out of the cab and when I got in front of the house, there was this bundle just by the curb, and so I thought it was yours, and I brought it along thinking maybe you'd give me a little something for a cup of …"

Her lush lip curled. "Just another panhandling stall," she said. "What's in your bundle, old newspapers?"

"I don't know, lady, I just picked it up. I didn't look."

She flared at Fred. "You're a fool to fall for a gag like

this! I've a good mind to report you."

He tried to explain, but I interrupted. I said, "Listen, lady, this ain't no angle I'm working. You can open the bundle and see what's in it, if you don't believe me."

She snatched the bundle and ripped the paper open. She handed it back to me.

"Well, it's not mine, anyway," she snapped and slammed the door. I heard the safety chain put on again.

"I could've sworn she dropped it," I said.

The doorman snorted. "Come on, grandpop. Get the hell outta here. You've made me enough trouble."

As we went down in the elevator, I took the shirt, the handkerchiefs and the tie from the torn paper and examined them.

"I guess I can use 'em, anyhow," I said.

"I'll take charge of 'em," he said. "Some other tenant dropped 'em and I'll find out who."

I didn't want it to be too easy for the greedy boor and I said I guessed I'd take them along with me. It ended, of course, with him taking the lot. He gave me a dime in a lordly fashion.

"Get yourself that cup of coffee," he said. "And don't try to get back here, grandpop. We don't allow beggars."

It would have been a pleasure to throttle the puppy, but I shuffled meekly out. The last shadow of a doubt I had was wiped out by what I'd learned.

I went to the nearest drugstore and telephoned Rafe Conner at his hotel. He answered sleepily, but snapped out of it when I told him I had found Stella Vardis.

"Didn't have time to call you before," I lied. "Meet me at Pennsylvania Station and we'll get right out to Scraffton."

"Where is she?"

I pretended not to hear. I said, "I'm to hell and gone

in the wilderness, so it may take me a little while to get there."

"I asked you where she was. What's all this about going to Scraffton Station, anyhow? She's not there, is she?"

"No, but her Wellington is."

"Talk sense, will you, Mr. Bixby?"

"Every Napoleon's got his Waterloo—and his Wellington to give it to him."

"What's all this got to do with …"

"I thought you followed my explanation the other night. If you didn't see that the way to break Vardis is … well, I'll tell you on the train. Meet me at the Long Island Information desk."

He was still fuming, demanding to know where Stella Vardis was, when I hung up on him. I was feeling that, in truth, this was the best of all possible worlds by the time I reached the Long Island level of the Pennsylvania Station and saw Rafe Conner, scowling impatiently, waiting for me. A train was leaving for Scraffton in three minutes, so I refused to explain until we were aboard. He followed me unwillingly, protesting that it was a wild goose chase, but he followed. By the time our train left Jamaica, his scowl was gone.

"It's not the way I'd have pulled it, but it may be the smart stunt," he said. "If there is a hitch, I can step in and do it my way."

"I don't think there'll be a hitch," I said. "Incidentally, in case of trouble, I have a pistol for which I have no permit."

"Well, I don't know that," he said, settling back in his seat, a picture of placid calm, except for his eyes. I'd noticed before they were flint-like. Now they were polished flint that gleamed. He chewed his gum steadily.

"Remember one thing," I said. "You've promised to play it out my way. Under no circumstances can you call anyone else until it's over. I'm giving you your case, but I insist that one person goes free. And don't forget you've made the bargain."

"But if I have to call in the New York cops …"

"You can call them after it's all over. Tell them you had to move too fast and didn't have time before. It may be slightly illegal, but they won't kick too much as long as they get in on the credit for the arrests."

He frowned, but finally he said, "Okay, you're the doctor."

When we reached Scraffton Station, he telephoned for a plainclothesman to bring a police sedan. We dropped the man at the precinct house and then drove on to the big, rambling house with the white picket fence around it and the rose garden off to one side. We got out and went up the shaded walk. We looked at each other as I rang the bell. The detective's jaw was set. His mouth was a thin, grim line. I grinned at him.

"I wouldn't be surprised if what we're going to do is illegal."

"So's murder," he said.

I heard someone walking inside the house. I could tell by the step it was a woman. She opened the door. Her eyes widened slightly at seeing us.

We went into a large, cool living room and sat down. The woman said, "Now what is it, please?"

I glanced at Conner and he stood up. He put a fresh piece of gum in his mouth before he spoke.

"You'll have to come with us," he said.

"But why? I don't understand. What's happened?"

"Dr. Overhart," he said, "I'm arresting you for murder."

Chapter Fifteen

Ruth Overhart sat stunned. She tried to speak, but could only swallow convulsively. When at last words came, her voice sounded like something I had never heard. It was not a human voice.

"No ... no ... I don't know what you mean ..."

"The electric chair isn't a nice way to die," Rafe said. His voice was a sledge. "Make a clean breast, and you may get off with life. It's your only chance."

She shook her head dully. She turned to me. Her eyes were burning queerly.

"You know it's not so, Mr. Bixby. Tell him, please tell him. You've known me all my life."

"It's too late, Ruth. We know Dirck Wannerman's alive."

She stared at him with doomed and unbelieving eyes. Her hands were clinched like claws on the arms of her chair. Her voice was a harsh whisper.

"He's dead," she said. "I saw him buried."

Rafe got up. "You're wrong, lady, and we're going to show you just how wrong."

"I tell you I saw him ..."

I leaned forward. "We're going to take you to him, Ruth. We're going to show you what a fool he's made of you."

She went with us like a woman walking in her sleep. She did not speak all the way to New York. She did not lift her head even when we stopped in front of Mamie Bell's house.

I went in to get Tie and Gretchen Jones. We might need her, and Tie's a handy lad in case of trouble. They told me Mamie was out shopping. I was glad of that. I couldn't afford to realize how old I was just then. I made Tie go on down to the car while the girl and I delayed a few moments in her room.

"This is the blow-up," I told her. "There's one thing you've got to tell me before we go."

Her eyes were suspicious, icy, defiant.

"I can guess Stella Vardis made it possible for you, but ..."

She broke in. "Does it have to be now?"

I nodded. She said, "I hoped Tie and I ... I hoped it wouldn't have to end so soon."

"I've got to know why you did it," I said.

She told me then. It took only a few moments, and when she was done, she smiled wanly.

"They say an honest confession's good for the soul, but I only feel tired," she said.

I took her down to the car. Ruth and Conner were in the front seat. Tie and I rode in back with Gretchen between us. Ruth didn't even glance around as we got in. Gretchen held Tie's hand tightly all the way, but I pretended not to notice.

When we got to the apartment house on Northern Avenue, the hallman wasn't anywhere in sight. That was a break. If he'd been there, we'd have had to take him with us. Rafe still wanted to call the New York police, but I held him to his promise.

"Well, anyhow," he said, "I'm glad you heard their radio."

We rode the automatic elevator to the seventh floor. I told Tie to keep the women in the lift, and I followed Rafe Conner the couple of steps to the door marked 7-A. He drew his revolver and held it against his leg so it couldn't be seen from the apartment unless the door was fully open. I pressed against the wall out of sight from the door and held my gun ready in my pocket, but I didn't draw. Then Conner rang the bell.

It seemed a long time before we heard a woman's clicking step inside. The door was opened a crack on the safety chain, and Rafe spoke.

"The super sent me up, Mrs. Lewis. There's something wrong with some of the radios, and I've got to check on all the aerials."

"There's nothing wrong with ours," she snapped.

"I know, but the super's trying to locate the short. That's what he thinks is causing the trouble."

There was a long pause and then she said, "All right, but make it snappy."

The chain rattled as it was loosened and she opened the door. Conner stepped quickly forward. The startled woman tried to slam the door, but he caught it on his shoulder. He pushed her aside and dashed into the apartment with his gun waist high.

I was on his heels and gave the woman a gentle shove toward a couch. I said, "This is a pinch, baby." I hoped I sounded enough like a movie detective to impress her.

She sat down as though stupefied. I closed the door and stood ready while Rafe went into the bedroom, then to the kitchen and even opened the bathroom door to see if anybody was there. As he closed it, he turned back to us.

"He's not here," he said. "Let the others in and we'll wait."

Stella Vardis stood up. Her voice trembled. "You can't do this!"

"We're doing it," Rafe said.

"What do you want? What have you come breaking in here for?"

"You know already," he said. "Sit down."

"I won't, I …"

"Sit down if you want to stay in one piece! Listen, baby, a couple of men have been murdered and you're in it up to your ears. So don't try any injured innocence."

She sat down weakly on the couch as I let the others in. A flash of recognition passed between Stella and Gretchen, but neither spoke. Ruth sat down in a chair like a woman drugged. Gretchen sat in a big easy chair, and Tie sat on the arm. He let his hand rest on her shoulder. She looked up at him once and tried to smile, but she couldn't. She was too near crying. I sat down against the wall, and Rafe put the safety chain back on the door before he sat down beside me.

"Just so Mr. Lewis won't walk in and surprise us," he said.

I'd expected Ruth to have hysterics when she saw Stella Vardis, but she did not seem even aware that the blonde or any of us were in the room.

"Miss Vardis," I said, "when will Mr. Wannerman be home?"

"Why ... he's dead, isn't he? The papers said ... My name's Lewis, Mrs. Lewis. Didn't you know I'd quit him to get married?"

Rafe broke in, "Come off it, sister. We've got that guy earmarked for the chair, and if you know what's good for you, you won't hold out on us."

She hesitated a moment, biting her lower lip. Then she said, "I thought I was through with that. I haven't seen him in ... Oh, a long time. Not since I got married."

Rafe glanced at me and nodded. I took my pipe out, filling it carefully, lighting it carefully, puffing slowly until it was drawing well, and then I said:

"History is a collection of lies that fools believe, but this isn't history yet, so let's have an end to lying and pretense. I'll start the ball of truth rolling, though that's a dangerous thing to do. Once a truth is set rolling through the world, you never can tell how many gilded monuments it will knock down. But I'll risk it. I will tell you exactly what happened."

I paused a moment, sucking on my pipe. Ruth Overhart sat like a woman hypnotized. Stella Vardis was staring at me with terror in her eyes. Tie was frowning, and Gretchen's face was strained and white.

"I'll tell you what happened first," I said, "and then I'll tell you how I know it happened. I will concede there are a few gaps I have filled by logical guesses, but none of these are essential to proving my thesis that Dirck Wannerman is guilty of two murders; that Ruth Overhart is guilty with him of at least one; that Stella Vardis probably had guilty knowledge of both."

I paused, but nobody spoke. I wondered whether Ruth Overhart or Stella Vardis would snap first under the strain.

"Dirck Wannerman was a smart criminal, but he wasn't original," I said. "He obviously got his idea from a fellow named Schwartz, who tried a somewhat similar crime in California in 1935. Schwartz committed suicide to escape arrest when he was cornered in the rooming house where he had previously set up a false personality which he assumed after his supposed death. Dirck Wannerman won't have a chance to commit suicide, though. When he walks through that door, he's started on the last lap to the electric chair.

"Wannerman's process for producing fine silk that never saw a silkworm was a swindle, of course. It was a smart swindle, though, and he played it to the hilt for every dollar it would bring. He planned to swindle his backer, the insurance company—and at least one of his accomplices.

"I admire the way he handled Nicky Pet and that shyster Sally Fiore. Anyone who ever read the newspapers was bound to know about them, and Wannerman was shrewd to pick them for his suckers. New York's most powerful gangster would hardly think anyone would dare try to swindle him. And Dirck Wannerman landed them by the first rule of a successful con man: always make your sucker think he's going to get rich by gypping somebody else. He didn't ask Fiore for money; didn't ask him even to help obtain a backer. All he wanted Fiore to do was to handle the incorporation of a company to finance the final stages of developing his process for commercial production.

"Since Wannerman didn't try to get money to back the silk experiments from him, Sally Fiore naturally figured that here was a chance to get in on the ground floor of a gold mine. Oh, he was very smart about it; very smart, indeed. He and Nicky Pet made Wannerman actually produce silk by his process before they forced him to accept Nicky Pet as his sole backer. If Wannerman is as smart as I think he is, 'forced' is the proper word.

"Nicky Pet and Fiore didn't know they were getting merely a demonstration of rudimentary parlor magic. I confess that this is one of the slight gaps I am filling with a guess, but I feel sure it is a perfect guess. (1) Wannerman took them to his laboratory and showed them a vat filled with clear water. Then he put in his raw materials. What it was doesn't matter, though probably it was stuff that would dissolve. Then he put in something to make the water opaque and something to make it seem that the process was at work. My guess would be coloring matter, soap and some harmless chemicals to make it smoke and look mysterious. And then, when they were properly impressed, he reached in and began pulling out the finished product, dripping wet, but still obviously fine silk. My guess is that, behind a cardboard lining of the vat, he had wound this silk around and around the inside of the vat, holding it in place with tabs. Working on the same principle, some magicians are able to pull yards and yards of silk from an apparently empty silk hat.

"Whether this was exactly the way he did it doesn't really matter, of course. The *modus operandi* is not vital to proving my thesis. It is sufficient that I can prove Wannerman obtained, over a period of time, thirty thousand dollars from Nicky Pet to finance his experiments. When he realized that Nicky was becoming impatient and that the gangster would soon be demanding a showdown, he turned to the second step of his very shrewd plan.

"He made over his life insurance to Ruth Overhart. I don't think she had actually put up the money she claimed and which, of course, she had his note to prove, but that is beside the point. It is incontrovertible that she was his accomplice. The plan was that they should fake his death in an apparently accidental fire which destroyed the laboratory and that she should then collect the life insurance, communicate with him to some blind address when she had the money and join him to live happily ever after.

"What Ruth, poor fool, didn't know was that Wannerman was taking her for a buggy ride. To quiet any jealousy or suspicions she may have had, he pretended that he had given up Stella Vardis. And Miss Vardis pretended that she had quit her career and was planning to get married. On weekends or whenever else he could get away from home without arousing comment, Wannerman came up here to Northern Avenue with Miss Vardis and built up the false personality of David P. Lewis, a travelling salesman, and his wife, who sometimes went with him. The result was that their absence or presence, no matter how irregular, would not cause comment.

"Everything was ready for the killing then. I don't suppose we will ever know who the murdered man we found in the laboratory really was. Not that it matters. You can be hanged as dead for killing John Doe as for murdering the President of the United States. Still, it is my guess that our John Doe was a bum from the Bowery, somebody picked for the slaughter because he resembled Wannerman's build, somebody no one in the world would ever miss.

"I don't know how he was enticed to Long Island. A cushy job was promised him, probably. I believe he was held prisoner, bound and gagged, in Dr. Overhart's home for several days until they were ready to kill him, but I tell you frankly I can't prove it. But wherever he came from, however he got into the laboratory, he was murdered by Wannerman and Dr. Overhart, and I can prove that.

"Dirck Wannerman may have been the actual killer, but I believe it was you, Ruth, because your medical knowledge would make a slip less likely. It doesn't matter which of you actually shot that bubble of air into the helpless man's vein, though. You're both equally guilty under the law. Incidentally, I wonder about one thing, Ruth. Did you kill him in the laboratory or did you murder him in your home and then carry the corpse there?"

I paused, but she sat frozen as though she had not heard a word I'd said. Stella Vardis was twisting a handkerchief in her lap. She sat staring at me as a bird stares at a snake.

"But I'm getting ahead of my story," I said. "As perfect as it was, Wannerman's plan hit a snag. An old man's conceit impels me to put on the record that I deduced the nature of this snag and everything else about it except the primary motive behind it. I was told what that motive was only today, but I would have you note—again an old man's conceit—that while it is interesting, the motive is not vital to the proof of my thesis.

"The primary motive I have mentioned was merely this: while Wannerman was living in California, around 1935, he ran an oil stock swindle. I don't know how successful he was, but he did wipe out at least one man. That man paid as fully for his folly as any fool can pay: he died for it. The shock was too much for a weak heart. He left a daughter without a sou to be cared for by relatives. She grew up and came to New York to make her way, but she never forgot the man who killed her father.

"I did not know this motive until today, but the instant I learned that Stella Vardis sang at the Golden Mirror, I knew how the snag in Wannerman's plan developed as surely as though I'd been there.

"Wannerman came down to the Golden Mirror to see Miss Vardis, and the girl from California saw him. He didn't recognize her, of course. She naturally tried to find out about him, and it would hardly have taken a master at the art of pumping to learn that Miss Vardis' heavy sugar daddy—I believe that is the phrase—was a big scientist who was developing a process for making silk. Oh, it was indiscreet of Miss Vardis, of course, but what woman ever is discreet if by indiscretion she can lord it over a more attractive girl?

"Now the girl from California was nobody's fool. She knew Wannerman was a swindler and, as I suspected the moment I guessed she was in California in 1935, she remembered the Schwartz case. So it was natural that she should deduce that this silk process was a swindle, too. And what was more natural than that she should try to avenge her father by hurting Wannerman in the only way he could he hurt—by taking money from him?

"So she enlisted a couple of the petty crooks who hang around the Golden Mirror, Mickey Carr and Anthony-I-forget-his-name. The money was all the motive they needed, and the girl saw her chance to get back the money stolen from her father and, what I believe was more important to her, to avenge him. So they blackmailed Wannerman. They threatened to reveal his silk process was a fake unless he paid off. I believe this threat forced Wannerman to put his murder plan into effect earlier than he expected. Miss Vardis' sudden departure from her apartment indicated that to me.

"That isn't really important, though. What is important is that Wannerman made an appointment with the blackmailers to pass the money in the women's lavatory on a certain train at a certain moment just a few minutes before the train reached Scraffton Station. The arrangement was made by telephone and a sign and countersign agreed on.

"When Mickey Carr stepped into the lavatory for the meeting, Wannerman was either waiting or followed on his heels. And he cut Carr's throat with a Gurkha knife which he flushed out the toilet. As Carr fell, strangling on his own blood, unable to cry out, Wannerman stepped quickly from the car. His clothes must have been spattered with blood. So he jerked a door open as the train slowed for the curve at Doran's Woods and jumped off. The sand piled along the embankment there broke his fall and he came home through the woods without being observed. It's within sight of our houses.

"I do not know exactly how Wannerman managed to cut Carr's throat in the narrow lavatory. He must have grabbed him from behind and held him for the moment it took to dig the knife in his victim's throat and slice the jugular. Or he might … but it is enough that it must have been possible, because he did it. And he must have jumped off at Doran's Woods because he was seen aboard the train, because he did not arrive at Scraffton Station and because the curve at Doran's Woods was the only place he could have jumped off without being seen and without certain injury.

"I grant you that it would be difficult—I would even make book on it being impossible—to convict Wannerman of the murder of Mickey Carr on this evidence we have, no matter how certain we are he committed the crime. But we don't need to convict him of Carr's killing. We can convict him of the murder of John Doe. And one electrocution is usually sufficient punishment for any murderer.

"All of which brings us back to the laboratory. Wannerman is there alone, fixing the last arrangements for the fire. Dr. Overhart comes over to our house for an alibi just in case there is ever the faintest suspicion. Sally Fiore arrives for a showdown. And Wannerman sets off the fire and flees. I suspect he had a car—probably a drive-yourself machine—parked nearby and so he was able to motor calmly away to New York to assume the personality of David

P. Lewis while his wife screamed hysterically that he was dead. He may have gotten away in some other manner, but however he escaped, the fact remains that he murdered the man whose burned cadaver was found in the wreckage of the fire.

"It was unfortunate for Wannerman and his accomplices that the watchman forgot his raincoat and came back for it. If he hadn't, the fire wouldn't have been discovered until too late for any clue to arson to have been found. If that had not been discovered, there doubtless would have been no autopsy to reveal how the poor devil died. It would have been too obvious to everyone that 'Mr. Wannerman' had been burned to death in a laboratory accident.

"But the watchman did come back. The tacks and the bits of film that proved the fire was arson were found. So there was an autopsy that revealed the burned man had been murdered before the fire touched him. And my son discovered, though he didn't know it, the evidence that proved the dead man was not Dirck Wannerman.

"So Dirck Wannerman is going to die in the electric chair. The only chance you, Ruth, and you, Miss Vardis, have to escape dying with him is to confess and help us send him there."

I leaned back and looked from one woman to the other. Ruth Overhart was staring dully down at her hands clinched together in her lap.

"You're lying," she said. Her voice was toneless, parched. "You're telling lies."

Stella Vardis laughed shakily and lit a cigarette. She said, "You almost had me believing you for a minute. You do a swell act, but it won't go over. Even if all you say wasn't a lot of malarkey, you couldn't prove a tenth of it."

I knocked out my pipe slowly. I settled back more comfortably in my chair. I smiled at them.

"I will now prove it to you," I said. "The first links in the chain of evidence that's going to shackle Dirck Wannerman into the electric chair were his gas and electric bills. The gas bill was $2.40 and the electric bill was S4.67. They run about the same as my own bills—and I don't operate a laboratory where I work day and night trying to perfect a process for making silk. Those bills told me as surely as if they'd spoken that Dirck Wannerman's scientific toil was a fake. He probably sat out there reading the funny papers. Whatever he did in his lab, it was a cinch he wasn't doing any scientific research with gas and electric bills so small.

"This made me suspect the true importance of the note that was found in Mickey Carr's pocket, but I must confess that I did not become certain about the note until I had received corroborative evidence.

"The first corroboration I had was learning that Anthony-what's-his-name—I believe my son calls him 'Tuck Waist'—had demanded a large sum of money from the girl from California; a sum of money she and Mickey Carr were supposed to have received from someone else before he got his throat cut. This made me virtually sure. And I became positive when I learned she had been in California in 1935, and so undoubtedly knew about the Schwartz case. As clinching evidence, there was the fact that on the train she was reading a book with a title that began *SI* ... Under the circumstances, one would hardly guess that it was a treatise on Sin.

"These facts gave the note definite meaning. The stars and designs which my son describes as 'doodling' indicated that Mr. Carr had taken the note while telephoning.

"Mr. Conner and my son deduced the obvious meaning of most of the first line of the note: the ladies' lavatory of the smoker. They were baffled by *211*. It seemed apparent to me that these numerals were the time, 2:11 P.M., which was just four minutes before the train reached Scraffton. That interpretation would mean that Carr met Wannerman in the ladies' room at 2:11 and got his throat cut in ample time for Wannerman to jump off the train at the wooded curve.

"In the light of what I knew, the lines that followed seemed to me plainly a sign and countersign. *W*—which would be Wannerman—was to say, 'Looks like a hot Summer.' *A*—apparently standing for Answer—was the reply, 'Never gets this hot in Oshkosh.' Quite silly, I grant you, but no sillier than scores of other blackmail arrangements.

"As for the cryptic *NUTS*, that would seem to be Mr. Carr's very apt comment on the state of the world.

"But Wannerman had actually shown Nicky Pet and Sally Fiore a large quantity of fine silk pulled from his vat before his eyes. While this was one of the lesser points of my deduction, I was amused that my son did not see the logical explanation. Among the papers burned in Wannerman's wastebasket, he found a scrap of bill on which he made out part of a firm name: ... LEWITE & COH ... On this minor point, chance helped those with perception enough to help themselves, as chance usually does. I remembered that among the passengers on the train when Carr had his throat cut was a Mr. Smythe, who was connected with the Fifth Avenue silk firm of Hepplewite & Cohen. This explains whence came the silk Wannerman showed to Nicky Pet, as the District

Attorney will doubtless find.

"Now to a much more important link in the chain. The first theory about the fire was, naturally, that Wannerman had set the blaze to collect fire insurance and had been caught in it. But Wannerman had no insurance. Why, then, should he have set fire to the laboratory?

"The first answer that suggested itself was, of course, that he had planned to tell Nicky Pet all his scientific data had been lost in the fire and so he couldn't go on with developing the process. But this would hardly have satisfied Nicky Pet for the loss of twenty thousand dollars. It didn't seem logical that Wannerman would have been fool enough to think it would, either.

"But the dental charts proved Wannerman was the dead man. The charts tallied with the burned man's teeth to the smallest detail. It was a perfect, incontrovertible identification.

"Then came the most important link of all: the dead man's ear. It was printed in the melted varnish on the laboratory cabinet. I got the student annual of Wannerman's college for the year he graduated. The photographs of him were old, but not too old to prove beyond the shadow of a doubt that the burned man was not Dirck Wannerman.

"For the print of the dead man's ear showed a full lobe. And Wannerman's photographs showed a lobeless ear.

"This meant that the identification by the dental charts was false. That meant the dentist must have been his accomplice. It meant Dr. Ruth Overhart must have prepared a chart of the victim's teeth, possibly doing some work on them while he was a helpless prisoner, in order to establish the false identity.

"It was all very shrewdly done, Ruth, but you and Wannerman made the mistake of being too careful. I suppose you took that Gurhka knife from my house because you feared the police might trace a knife you bought. And you figured that they couldn't trace such an old knife and it might make them suspect foreigners, too, didn't you? You'd have been a lot smarter if you'd risked having a knife traced. For using the Gurkha knife brought me into the mess."

I paused and looked at Ruth until she lifted her eyes to my face. Then I smiled mockingly. An edged jeer was in my voice as I went on.

"Don't you realize now you were a fool, Ruth? Don't you realize now that Dirck Wannerman never broke with Stella Vardis? He just told you he did, and all the time they were up here together laughing at you. And you with your mouse-colored hair, showing your age more every day, thought you could take him away from a beautiful woman like Stella Vardis?"

I threw back my head and laughed at her. Her mouth moved convulsively. In another moment, she'd snap.

Conner was hammering at her. "Don't you see he was going to ditch you once he got the money. He probably planned to kill you ..."

"That is quite right!"

We whirled to the sound. A man was standing in the bathroom door. He was covering us with a steady pistol. It had a silencer. He was smiling.

"Of course, I was going to kill her. You don't think I could stand living with her, do you?"

Stella Vardis stood up. She wasn't trembling now. She was pale, but her mouth was twisted in a brittle smile. Dirck Wannerman nodded toward Rafe.

"Get that flatfoot's gun," he said. "Frisk the others, too."

The blonde was careful she didn't get in the line of fire as she took Rafe's pistol, as she patted Tie's pockets.

Wannerman said, "Don't slight the Ancient Mariner. See if he's got his blunderbuss."

I had to chance a bluff. I blazed at him in senile rage. "If this damned fool of a detective had given me one, you wouldn't be standing there! I'd have filled you so full of holes by this time that they could use you for a sieve. And I'm not going to stand here like a ninny just to please you. I wash my hands of the whole mess and I'm going to sit down …"

I was turning as I spoke, not even glancing at Wannerman. I expected a bullet, but I had to risk it. I kept on talking as I took a shuffling step or so to a big chair and let myself down in it, grumbling and cursing.

"Go ahead and shoot and to hell with you. I'm sick and tired of the whole shooting match and my feet hurt. And that damned jackass that calls himself a detective …"

Stella Vardis was looking at Wannerman. I glanced at him, beetling my brows and glaring. He frowned uncertainly. I bent down and began taking off my shoes as I spoke.

"I've stood all I'm going to stand. Once I get these blasted shoes off my feet, your lady friend can search me all she damned well pleases and she's welcome to what she finds. And if you don't like it, just fire away and to hell with you. I'm seventy years old and I guess I won't be missing much. If ever I get my hands on that shoe clerk's neck …"

Wannerman laughed. "Take it easy, Methuselah, and maybe you won't get hurt."

The blonde gave him Rafe's gun and he said, "Get that cord out of the bedroom and tie him up. Truss up the young fellow, too."

I kept on grumbling and growling about my feet, about the stupidity of the detective who was too dumb to solve a case when I laid it in his lap. Wannerman seemed amused.

"You're pretty smart, Foxy Grandpa. I bet you'd have found me. Your bovine friend looked in the bathroom and never thought to look in the shower curtain. Of course, I'd have plugged him if he had."

"Go ahead and plug him now. You've got my permission."

His laugh was cold. The blonde had finished binding Tie's and Rafe's hands behind them.

"There's not much rope," she said. "What about the others."

"They've got enough to hang themselves already. Let 'em be. Go get your hat."

She went to the bedroom, and Wannerman stepped behind the big sofa. He said, "I'll stand here just in case any of you is fool enough to try to rush me. Now stand up, all of you, over against that inside wall."

The others obeyed, but I said, "Damned if I'll budge. My feet hurt, and you can kill me if you want to, but I'm not going to move."

"I'll make an exception for you, Methuselah. You may remain seated. But don't get any ideas …"

I bent over, rubbing my feet, muttering to myself. Rafe Conner stood livid against the wall. Ruth Overhart was staring at Wannerman with wild eyes. A sickly grin was frozen on Tie's face. Gretchen was standing beside him, holding his arm.

"I heard Foxy Grandpa's little bedtime story," Wannerman said, "and I don't mind telling you it's quite true. If I had time, I'd fill in a few of the unimportant gaps he mentioned. But Miss Vardis and

I really must be going ..."

He stood a moment, smiling at them. When he spoke again, his voice was as soft as velvet.

"So I must kill you all," he said. "Let them hunt for Mr. and Mrs. Lewis. I can't afford to have so many witnesses tell them it's Dirck Wannerman they want."

Ruth gasped. That was the only sound. Rafe was glaring at the killer. Tie wet his lips. Gretchen closed her eyes and held tightly to his arm. I heard Stella Vardis come back from the bedroom.

"Turn on the radio," Wannerman said. "Get loud music."

The program blared into the room. He stood there looking at us, smiling. The radio and the silencer would drown the shots. The smile faded from his thin lips. That was when Ruth began to babble.

"You can't, Dirck! Oh, for God's sake, you can't do this to me. You love me. You said you did. You told me ..."

"Once a sucker, always a sucker," he said.

"You said if I killed him for you ..."

He fired. The bullet struck her in the chest. A sickly surprise came over her face.

Stella Vardis was staring with her mouth open. Conner blurted, "And you're next when he's tired of you!"

Wannerman whirled on him. "You're wrong, big boy. You're next."

The blonde cried out. "Not any more, Dirck! We've got ..." She put her hand impulsively on his arm. He flung it back angrily. For an instant, he was half turned to the pleading woman.

I fired twice from the chair. The bullets spun him around. He was trying to raise his gun. I fired again. The bullet smacked into his face. After he fell, the blonde stood staring stupidly down at him awhile and then she fainted.

I could hear people yelling as I untied Rafe. Somebody started pounding at the door. Rafe grabbed me by the arm.

"That was my gun you used, Mr. Bixby. I stuck it in the chair and you used it. We'll have enough hell with these New York cops without having you caught with an illegal weapon."

Postscript

It was late at night before they let us go. There were the charges against Gretchen and Tie, but Tuck Waist discreetly swore that he'd never seen them before. The cab driver and the cops and the other tenants said they couldn't be sure. With all the hoopla Rafe was putting out about the heroic assistance we'd been in cracking the Wannerman case, it would have taken a nervy guy to swear they were crooks.

There was a homicide charge against me, of course, but the magistrate released me on my own recognizance and gave me a lot of ballyhoo from the bench. He said I'd be dismissed with a brass band and he'd lead it. There were a lot of photographers and reporters, and Rafe smeared a lot of credit on the D.A. and the New York cops, which didn't make anybody any tougher on us.

It was over at last, though, and I walked down the street with Tie and Gretchen. I was remembering something I had to do.

"We're going over to Jersey," Tie said. "We're going to keep going until we find somebody who'll marry us tonight. And you're coming too."

"Please," the girl said. "I won't feel we're really

married unless you're the best man."

I wouldn't go. There was something else I had to do. We stopped at a bar long enough for me to cash a check for Tie, and then they tumbled into a taxi. They were laughing. The last glimpse I had of them, he was kissing her.

Then I went to do the thing I had to do. Paula Wannerman had been waiting at the flat all day for me to call. Now I had to tell her about Tie. I dropped my nickel in the box. It seemed to me one of those times when you should ask a young lady to get drunk.

THE END

Asa Cyril Bordages was born on March 2, 1906, in Beaumont, Texas. He lived in Houston, Texas in the 1920s and moved to New York in 1932, where he became a feature writer for the *New York World Telegram*, marrying actress Gertrude Flynn in 1933. In 1941 Bordages authored a play, *Brooklyn, USA,* with screenwriter John Bright, featuring characters based on Murder, Inc. gangsters. It ran for 47 performances, and was revived in Hollywood in 2010. Bordages wrote two novels under his real name, and two more as Mike Teagle. He died on December 9, 1986, in Columbia, Knowlton Township, New Jersey, at the age of 80.

www.ingramcontent.com/pod-product-compliance
Lightning Source LLC
LaVergne TN
LVHW021811060526
838201LV00058B/3338